PROMPT CREATIONS (IN A PANDEMIC)
A Collection of Thirty-One Ultra Short Stories

By Phil Brackett

To Jennie, in recognition of her love and support, and because she's the only person who ought to receive a dedication on my first published work.

PREFACE

"So, what did you do during the pandemic?

"Well, I made a world."

* * *

I'm an English teacher by trade, at least that's how things started out for me twenty some years ago. I've taught, during my career, all manner of English classes, including Honors English classes and Freshman English classes. During the early years of my career, there were even a few school years when I was the Creative Writing teacher.

Eventually though, my career went off the rails a little bit when I got co-opted into different administrative duties in my school district, taking me further and further away from teaching English classes and more and more into other stuff. Don't cry for me; I'm doing fine. But, my history in teaching is a preface to the preface, I guess.

As an English teacher, I bought a book, probably more than fifteen years ago, of creative writing prompts, fifty percent of me thinking that I could use them in my writing classes to help my students become better writers, fifty percent of me thinking that I would use the prompts to get myself some creative writing practice. And over the years, I've used a few of the prompts that are in that book with students in my classes. Unfortunately, though, if I'm being honest with myself –previous to the pandemic– I'd under-utilized the book.

But then, the unthinkable happened.

During the early portion of the pandemic, during the lockdown and the virtual teaching and the uncertainty and the fear, I wrote. A lot. Daily. More than 700 pages of blog posts on a WordPress blog that I got going so I could express myself. Later, I looked back at those posts, as the pandemic started to become less difficult, and I recognized them as equal parts 1) coping mechanism and 2) I can't believe that I actually did something so amazing.

When I stopped the daily posts on the blog, I shifted to writing my first novel (more on that in the future, with any luck). But, as that work started to become a challenge and a drain on my spirit, I needed something else. So, later in 2020, as we were all coming to terms with the new reality, I realized that I had become a writer during the pandemic. But, with my novel frustrating me, and with the steam released that had driven my daily blog writing, I needed something else to satisfy the itch.

So, with a creative writing prompt book in my possession, and an itch to get back at the writing, I challenged myself to some ultra short creative writing. Just to be clear about what's going on here: what you are about to read in the pages that follow is a series of short fiction pieces that I wrote in response to a series of prompts from that book (The Writer's Book of Matches – ISBN: 158297411X). Over the course of seventy-nine days, between December of 2020 and February of 2021, I wrote these thirty-one stories, issuing the stories –usually in their first or second draft form– through my blog to a couple dozen people who found themselves with nothing better to do during that part of the pandemic than to read them and encourage me in my new endeavor.

The connection between many of these stories and my developing novel is that they take place in the world that I built during the early days of the pandemic. I hope you enjoy these stories; I especially hope that you like the stories set in that world, Bangor Springs. As often as I've said that my favorite fiction author is Stephen King, I must admit that Bangor Springs is my version of Derry, Maine.

During the pandemic, I was reaching out to people on the internet via my blog at iotmt.org and via social media, asking them to provide the numbers, to choose which of the prompts I would end up writing. These numbers, as they came in, determined my course. The number listed in the title of each of these stories corresponds to a page in that 'book of matches'. You'll also note that the stories are presented in reverse order – the ones I wrote last, you'll read first.

Whether any of these stories are any good is mostly irrelevant to me; the importance of the writing that I did during the start of the pandemic comes because the writing helped me to cope and it helped me to see myself as a writer. Inasmuch as I was afraid and stressed and unnerved and discombobulated during the whole ordeal, I also grew. For better or for worse –whether you like any of these stories or not– they will always be a part of my phoenix experience – rising from the ashes of what was, to become a better, new creature.

Prompt Creation #115 - 2/24/21

The worst part of knowing that someone has been in your home, has invaded your home, is not being sure of what they've done, exactly. For Donna Emelander, it was clear that –when she arrived home from work that day– someone had been in her home. Not because there was a massive mess, and not because there was a list of items missing from the home. Rather, in the middle of her living room, on the coffee table there, her laptop computer was arranged, next to a pad of paper. The manner of the arrangement was as striking as any of the elements of the scene, for everything had been laid perfectly in place. The pad of paper, its leftmost edge, ran perfectly parallel to the right edge of the laptop keyboard. The laptop was open, and its screen/lid had been set in a position for perfect viewing for the person to be seated at it.

For Donna.

The pencil, laid on top of the pad of paper, was in a position where it was at a perfect perpendicular to the edges of the pad, laid underneath the three words written on the pad, as if to underscore them. Donna couldn't help but smirk to look at that pencil, to think that it would be necessary to underline those three words with the presence of the pencil underneath them. She had an infinite string of questions to ask of the person who'd done all of this, but she wasn't going to get to ask those questions of the person who'd invaded her home, just to set her belongings painstakingly in their positions.

Donna had been standing in a position of review, over the entire scene, for the better part of ten minutes. She was going through the questions that she had in her mind. She was trying to come to conclusions about who might have been responsible for something like this. She was concerned about the level of OCD that might be bubbling inside of a person who would set up a laptop, a pad of paper, and a pencil in such a way. Was someone with that level of compulsion still here, in the home at this very moment? How close are compulsive people and murderous people, in the grand scheme of things?

Donna's dog, Sassy, was lying in the corner of the living room, head down on its paws, a silent witness most likely to the person who'd been responsible for all of this, but without a damn word to say on the matter. Instead of looking for her dog to start spouting any words of wisdom in this instance, Donna looked back at the pad of paper.

Check your email.

Donna decided to sit, because she didn't really know what to think and she thought that she might as well be comfortable trying to come up with the answers. The yellow legal pad, on which the note was written, had come from her kitchen, from the drawer where she kept spare paper and notebooks and writing utensils. The laptop was, most likely, fetched from her office on the other side of the house and set up here on the coffee table. Every fiber of Donna's being wanted to call the police, for this was certainly something that the police ought to be investigating. Would she foul the 'crime scene' by touching the keys on the laptop? Would she ruin important physical evidence by disturbing what the invader had set up here? Donna didn't know, but she didn't really feel like there was much of a crime to report, at the moment.

Truth be told, however, Donna didn't need her laptop to check her email.

Donna got back up again, in a huff, deciding to leave the note and the laptop on the coffee table and return to the kitchen. Donna normally entered her home through its back door, which opens directly onto the kitchen from the back porch. Returning there, to the kitchen, she fished her cell phone out of the side pocket of her purse, and swiped into it, to be able to access her email on the phone itself. There, in the inbox, were emails about her credit card payment being due, and emails about switching her auto insurance to Geico. Donna scrolled through the list of emails that she'd yet to delete or archive from her inbox, until she scrolled down to an email whose subject line read,

"THIS IS THE EMAIL THAT YOU'RE LOOKING FOR".

Donna tapped on the message, and it opened up on the screen of her cell phone. It read:

Donna, here you are again, reading a message from me. Twice in one day! Lucky you, huh?!?! And look, this message is already longer than the first one was!!!

At least, by early indications, the author has some sense of humor, Donna thought.

Let me get to the point. The truth of the matter is this — I am a long-lost cousin of yours — the youngest son of your mother's oldest brother. We've never met, because my father and your mother were estranged and living some great distance apart.

It was certainly news to Donna that her mother had an older brother. Donna's mother had always described herself as the oldest of her siblings. Donna stopped to think about her mother and this new revelation, before continuing on in reading the email.

The reason for the estrangement between my father and your mother has always been a mystery to me, and my father –the uncle that you've never met, to my knowledge– died about a year ago. Since his death, I've been contemplating trying to get in touch with you, to see if there might be a way that we could meet.

I know that breaking into your home seems like a strange way for me to introduce myself, and I can't honestly explain why I did it, except to say that I was wanting something a little more personal for the both of us. I hope that this hasn't been too creepy, and I would certainly understand if meeting me might be the last thought on your mind right now.

However, if you're interested, I'm actually not that far away right now. I've left a map on your front porch swing (the old-fashioned kind of map) that will lead you on a five-minute walk to where I am waiting to see whether or not you show up to meet me. I'll leave the choice up to you.

Donna checked the sender email address, which didn't really give any information at all: 'skinnydee2729@gmail.com'. The email had only been in Donna's inbox for about a half-hour, so the whole situation had a kind of a live quality to it. Was she going to go out to her front porch, to grab a map that would lead her on a walk? Was she going to go out to her front porch to grab a piece of garbage that someone had left on her porch?

Instead, Donna did what she probably should have done twenty minutes ago. She backed out of her

email app, pulled up the numeric keypad in the
Phone app, and dialed 9-1-1.

Prompt Creation #124 - 2/22/21

Carl Lottsman, as far as magicians go, never quite arrived as a 'professional'. When one thinks of the term 'professional', it stirs up images of success and prestige and financial stability — Carl never had any of those as the result of pursuing being a magician, at least not to my knowledge. By all accounts, he was barely able to make enough money to pay the rent that his mother was forcing him to pay, on account of him living in her basement up until the age of twenty-three, with the work that he was able to find as a magician.

If you think about it, chances are you've never hired a magician before, have you? What would a person hire a magician for in the first place? Entertainment, most likely. Carl's problem was that he had never been very entertaining. If he had been, word of mouth may have assisted him in drumming up new business via the referrals of his previous business clients. But, that never ended up working for Carl.

Maybe, if he'd had more time.

As far as prestige is concerned, when one is trying to make it as a 'professional' magician, prestige and fame come to mean the same thing. Carl never became a famous magician, considering his stale repertoire of card tricks that he'd learned from YouTube videos, sleight-of-hand tricks that he'd learned from books he'd purchased at used book stores, and the rarely entertaining transformation tricks that he was able to perform, thanks to the props and gizmos that he bought on the internet, props and gizmos sold to struggling schmucks who had visions of fame and prestige dancing around in their mostly empty brains. It wasn't that Carl was incapable of putting any number of these tricks together to make a half-hour's worth of 'entertainment', according to the research that I've done. Unfortunately for him, he just lacked the theatrical talent to sell his show to an audience, to make them believe that he was magical.

It's the theater of a magic show that makes it, well, magical.

Carl had only ever on one occasion accomplished anything during a magic show that had ever impressed anyone. I should know; I was there that day, and I remember being impressed. I remember everyone present being impressed — at least initially. In the days that have passed since that sunny afternoon, in the backyard of the McCormac residence over on Belmont Avenue, I've become a bit of an expert on the events that lead Carl Lottsman to his fate.

The story goes something like this.

Carl had been hired by Mrs. Candice McCormac to be a source of entertainment at her son's eighth birthday party. The party took place on May 16th of 2015. Young Ron McCormac's birthday was actually May 19th, but Tuesday birthday parties are much harder to plan and pretty poorly attended. The last time I spoke with Candice, she was still consumed by a lot of grief, but she allowed me to interview her anyway, in the hopes that it might help. She was willing, back then, to do just about anything, if there was a chance that it might help.

To think, Ron would be a teenager these days.

Carl was set to perform at three that afternoon, after the cake and ice cream but before the piñata and the presents. I was there that afternoon because my daughter, Sheila, was one of Ron's third grade classmates. I stood in the back, with a few of the other parents who had chaperoned their children to this event. We all ended up —each of us parents— being interviewed as witnesses, during the subsequent investigation by the FBI. As far as I know, I'm the only witness who has become obsessed with what actually happened, however.

Carl's show started with the usual amateurish crap, precisely what one would have expected to see. He separated links in a chain from each other. He pulled a pigeon from a hat and set it free into the warm afternoon air. He made the ball underneath the cups disappear.

Whoopdeedoo.

The fact that these tricks were failing to impress a group of a half-dozen parents, standing behind their youngsters, wasn't the worst part. These tricks were failing to impress the youngsters themselves. And, while adults know better than to magnify the awkwardness of the situation by voicing their displeasure and boredom, children have no such filters developed in their minds. Their frustrations and apathy came right out their eight-year-old mouths, and Carl was starting to look pretty desperate, as I remember things. Fortunately for him, he'd almost reached his contracted show-length, as I ended up learning after the fact. One more trick and we'd all be released from this torture. We were all looking forward to watching Young Ron flail around, blind-folded with a stick in his hand and a piñata in the air — after Carl's miserable performance, nothing was likely to be more difficult to watch.

Ron never ended up taking a single swing at that piñata, though.
Instead, Carl –in classic magician fashion– ended up needing a volunteer from the audience for his last trick, and if you've never seen this before, it's normally the birthday child who gets volun-told into being that on-stage guest. Carl called Ron up to the area in front of the children, where he'd performed all of his previous tricks. Carl had Ron lay down on a folding table in front of the audience, and Carl draped a large piece of black cloth over Ron's body.

The whole thing was setting up to be the classic levitation pièce de résistance.

Unfortunately, Ron did a bit more than levitate.

In retrospect, I remember people in the audience, children and adults alike, being impressed that Ron was apparently floating above the table where he'd been previously laying. I even remember Carl looking inspired and excited. But, the problem was that Ron didn't just levitate. He rose. First, by a few inches, and then by a couple of feet, and then even higher still. Of course, we all thought that it was part of the show, Ron climbing higher and higher into the warm afternoon sky. At the point when Ron was about seventy feet in the air, and the draped cloth that was lying atop his body came off and drifted down to the ground, the children in the audience –Ron's classmates and friends and cousins– all jumped to their feet and cheered.

Quite impressive.

The problem, of course, was that Ron never came back down. He rose higher and higher until he was out of sight. Even then, the children were amazed, although some of the parents started to look back and forth at each other, wondering how this could possibly have been the final act of a magic show that was otherwise childish in its previous level of difficulty. Many of those parents started looking to Carl, to check what was going on across his face. It was there that those adult audience members saw the confusion of a young man who didn't seem to understand what he'd just done.

Some of the parents ushered the children off to get them involved in something to distract them, while other adults went to Carl and to Candice to try to figure out what had just happened.

You can probably imagine the rest of the story.

Carl was eventually convicted on federal kidnapping charges. He's been in a prison in Pekin, Illinois for going on four years. He never assisted his defense attorney in his own defense. He seemed to have on his face, every time I saw him after that, leading up to the day of his sentencing, a bewildered look on his face — I just don't think that Carl really could have told anyone, honestly, what happened that day. Whether or not that made him guilty of a federal crime, it was certainly hard to argue with the consequences of his actions.

Candice is still, according to reports, imagining that her son might return home one day. I haven't seen her or heard from her since the trial. And here I am, still trying to make sense of the whole thing, so tormented with the events of that day that I can't help but pour over the details, time and time again, hoping that it might occur to me what really happened.

Where did Ron McCormac go?

Prompt Creation #157 - 2/19/21

"What do you mean? What does 'our demographic has changed' actually mean?"

Ray was furious. He couldn't ever remember being so mad in all of his life. Did these people know who they were dealing with? Rockin' Ray Reed was a radio broadcast legend, and legends demand a certain amount of appropriate respect.

This was not how it was going down. Way low on the respect-o-meter, in Ray's opinion.

"Ray. Listen. We love you, man. Everyone at this station loves you. You've been the lifeblood of this place for decades. But, you can't argue with the numbers. Our demographic has changed, and we've not changed with them, to be able to keep our market share. We used to be the most popular radio station in Maine, according to the Nielsen ratings, but now we're not even in the top five."

Desmond Smith was probably Ray's least favorite person on the planet, and Ray tended to dislike anyone else at the studio that he ever saw in Desmond's presence. Desmond was small, and wiry, and his concern about the art coming out of the radio station was nil. If Rockin' Ray had a dollar for every time that Desmond had said the word 'Nielsen' in his presence, he'd be able to keep the radio station running –through the charitable donation of those dollars– well into the next decade. Above anything else, Ray Reed considered himself to be an artist, and he didn't have a lot of patience for people trying to make money off of his art, at the expense of his art.

"You know, Desmond, I don't really have time to listen to you, foaming at the mouth about ratings. I'm on the air in like three minutes and I haven't done a mic check yet. If you'll excuse me, my dude."

Ray started to walk away, mostly to keep from cleaning Desmond's clock, but that skinny little punk called right after him, his words striking Ray in the back like a coward's bullet.

"Change is coming, Ray, like it or not. You either get on the bus, or you get run over by the bus, my dude."

The eighty percent of Ray that wanted to turn around, walk right up to Desmond, and start beating on him, only to end up stopping when several nearby witnesses decided to pull him off of the sad brat, was somehow vetoed by the twenty percent of him that thought that spending his golden years as a prisoner in the State of Maine Department of Corrections, doing a dime for assault & battery, was probably a bad way to go out. Ray kept walking down the hall, opened the door to his radio booth, and walked in.

He sat down at his desk, across from his assistant, Parker, who was wearing the same 'Ramones' t-shirt that he always seemed to be wearing when he was at the station, and tried to catch his breath and calm himself. While he was focusing on happy thoughts and slowing his breathing, Ray looked over at Parker. For as long as Parker had been his assistant, Ray was fairly certain that Parker had never listened to a single song by the Ramones, but he'd heard –on more than one occasion– OneDirection melodies coming from Parker's airbuds, or whatever those little white things were called that Parker always had stuck in his ears.

"Sound check?" Parker asked, oblivious to Ray's heightened emotional state.

"Yeah, sure thing, kid."

Rockin' Ray went through the sound check that he'd performed thousands of times in his life — it was second nature to him, like breathing. Then, Parker told him he'd be live in about thirty seconds, when the current song finished playing. Ray took the opportunity to try to figure out what he was going to have to say during his first radio intro spiel.

"Welcome to the night shift everyone, this is Rockin' Ray Reed, comin' at you live from the WIRK radio studios in Augusta. You're in my world now. Tonight, just because I'm in the mood, we'll be starting off with some back-to-back Stones, because everyone needs a little more Jagger in their life."

Ray pressed a couple of buttons on the dashboard at his desk, the ones that would cue up a couple of his favorite hits from one of his favorite bands, and then he leaned over to his coffee mug, knowing that he would have at least a few minutes to sneak across the hall, over to the lounge, to grab some of the sludge that passed for coffee in this joint. He found his mug, where he always left it, next to his dashboard. He wondered when the last time was that he'd actually given the mug a good washing, deciding that his memory –at this late stage of his life– was probably not good enough to remember back that far, and banished the thought from his mind.

"I'll be back in a sec, Parker. Catch you on the flip side."
Ray stuck his head out in the hall, to check to make sure that Desmond Smith wasn't still out there. Finding that the coast was clear, he crossed the hall, and headed over to the lounge.

The double-burner Bunn coffee maker could conceivably keep two full pots of coffee warm and ready at the same time. After all, it was a restaurant-grade coffee machine. But, on this particular evening, the coffee maker was keeping a totally empty pot entirely too warm –baking the coffee remnants on the bottom of the glass– and another pot which was far more empty than full was being kept alive on the bottom burner of the machine. Ray grabbed what he could out of that last pot, and shut the machine off on his way out of the lounge, heading back to his office.

As he returned to his desk, Parker flashed him a three and a five with his right-hand fingers, which meant that Ray was going to be live in thirty-five seconds. Ray sat down, sipped the coffee — what it lacked in taste and quality it more than made up for in temperature — and prepared to take the broadcast back from the Stones.

"Ladies and Gents out there in Candyland, we're going to play a game tonight. You see, your friend and charming host, Rockin' Ray, has been told by certain managerial personnel at the radio station that he needs to modify his playlist because the listeners aren't happy. So, if you are listening out there and you think that's a bunch of hog-wash, ol' Rockin' Ray Reed is asking you to call in during these back-to-back hits from The Doobie Brothers, to let me know how much you appreciate the show. Startin' off with China Grove and then moving into Listen to the Music, I'd love to hear from you."

Ray dialed up the songs, and then he waited for the calls to start rolling in. He was going to record everyone of those calls, and then he was going to strap Desmond Smith to a chair with half a roll of duct tape and he was going to force that slimy worm to listen to every one of the calls, coming in from all of those people who would help Ray tell Desmond where he could stick his Nielsen ratings.

And so, Ray waited for those first calls to start rolling in.

Prompt Creation #111 - 2/17/21

Beatrice hated going to see her rheumatologist more than she hated any other chore, any other experience on this planet. If you can imagine being in a car, traveling at highway speeds, headed for a cliff, with no brakes and no other means of stopping the car or steering it in any other directions, and then to have someone, running along the side of the car, sticking their head in the window only to let you know that you are one mile from the cliff, that you are three-quarters of a mile from the cliff, that you are half-a-mile from the cliff, that you are five hundred yards from the cliff, then you might come to understand how annoying and futile and frustratingly infuriating Beatrice's visits to the rheumatologist were for her.

While she was not the only person in the world suffering from the debilitating effects of arthritis, she was a member of a smaller subset of arthritic people in the world who was recognized internationally as an artist whose career was going to be prematurely ended because of arthritis. Her fellows all over the world knew who she was, and knew how profound her artistry could be. They knew that she'd been diagnosed with arthritis, and they knew that she was –ever so slowly– becoming less and less capable as an artist because of the disease.

Even then, from that subset of people, Beatrice was a member of an even smaller subset of arthritic artists who felt as if they'd yet to hit their peak.

For it's most certainly one thing for a person to take their car off a cliff when they've 'had a good life' or when they're 'going out on a high note', but Beatrice –and don't you dare ever call her 'Betty', if you know what's good for you– was sure that she'd not yet accomplished her greatest art. She was sure that she still had work to do.

But the clock was ticking.

And visits to the rheumatologist were really just wasted time — why check the game clock when you still need to get to the other end of the field?!?!

Beatrice had been recognized, ever since she was eleven years old, as a prodigy on the violin. Her early teachers and musical instructors had recognized it in her, and her professors at Juilliard had been impressed by her to the point of finding themselves incapable of having much to teach to the young lady, despite their employment at one of the top music schools in the world. The one thing that Beatrice did get out of her educational experience at Juilliard was a solid development in composition. It was one thing for Bea –the only nickname that she allowed for people to use around her– to be able to play what other people, other composers had written, but she'd developed, as an adult, a desire to be the greater artist, capable of playing the violin and also writing music for it.

In school, and for the years to follow the end of her formal education, Beatrice wrote music as the vehicle for advancing her musical expertise. She started with writing pieces for the violin as a solo instrument, and was soon not at all challenged by doing that. Then, she wrote for string ensembles, and then for chamber orchestras, and then for full orchestras — each time, she took on the additional challenge that more advanced levels of composition offered, eventually mastering each challenge.

But, as one might expect, rheumatoid arthritis was taking its toll on both of Bea's musical endeavors.

The writing of musical composition, whether one does it by hand in musical notation on paper, or through the use of software on a computer, is like any creative art, especially those of a highly granular level of detail: a certain amount of manual dexterity is incumbent on the artist. In Beatrice's mind, a mind that envisioned that her ability to play music would probably outlast her ability to write music, any old dolt could play music. She had only recently been challenged, only recently found a level of satisfaction in the creative nature of musical composition.

But have you seen what arthritis can do to one's finger joints?!?!

For Bea, who'd been spending most of her time as a composer with a pencil and notebooks full of filled composition paper, she'd recently been forced to learn how to compose music on a computer. This wasn't the way that she'd grown to love writing music, so she didn't really take to it very well. And, it wasn't a technology thing, either — Bea used computers for others purposes and had no problems using a computer in general. It was just that she didn't want to have to make these changes.

She didn't feel that she should have to make these changes. But, the arthritis begged to differ with her.

She really just needed enough time to finish her last piece, a piece that she'd been working on now for almost two years. She started the work in the hopes of beating the clock, of beating the disease. Beatrice devoted as much time to the composition as she could manage, between playing as a guest soloist for this symphony or that one, between her obligatory symposiums and media appearances. She probably would have finished it already, if it weren't for her life being so busy and hectic.

And now, only about a hundred yards to the cliff.

Prompt Creation #139 - 2/15/21

Normally, I don't see much of anything, which isn't to say that I don't see things, because I certainly do. I certainly have. But, what I mean to say is that I don't normally see anything that's worth getting excited over.

I've seen the inside of thousands of apartments and condos and penthouses. I've seen how opulent they are — how about that: a window washer using a word like 'opulent'. I'll bet you weren't expecting that. The presuppositions we hold in our heads about different occupations, and hence, the people who hold them.

Window washing is probably not the best use of my full set of talents, I'll agree. If I had my wish, I'd probably be a famous writer of some kind. But, as my mother used to always say, whenever I had my head in the clouds as a child, "Wishes don't pay the bills, my Danny boy." So, instead, I'm a window washer in San Diego, CA. I like the job a lot, for reasons that might seem pretty obvious, when you think about it. It's pretty simple work, so it's easy to be good at it. My parents raised me to do whatever I was doing to the best of my ability, and they impressed on me how valuable it is to others when your service to them is top-notch. It's also amazingly fruitful work — by which I mean that I make more money than most menial laborers.

The one thing about window washing that I've not been able to find in any other job, the one thing about it that keeps me excited, day after day and month after month, is the thrill of it. Sometimes, I just stop my washing for a second, and I turn around on the platform, just to enjoy the views that aren't views of eighty-inch wall-mounted televisions or dining room tables that probably cost more than any car I've ever owned. Those views, sometimes of the San Diego Bay or Point Loma, sometimes of the Peninsular Ranges, sometimes of the Palomar Observatory, those views are beautiful and breath-taking in a way that will always excite me. I used to try to capture those views with my phone, but you have no idea how hard it is to try to find your phone after you've dropped it off the side of a three-hundred-foot tall building.

These days, I just capture the views with the camera of my memory, leaving my phone in my pocket.

Speaking of memory, it's not always panoramic vistas and luxurious living spaces that I end up seeing. Like I said before, I've seen some things. The fact of the matter is this — you'd be surprised how many people think that, by living hundreds of feet in the air, you don't need to invest in window treatments of any kind. Would it be so hard to get some shades installed, or a nice set of venetian blinds? I guess I'm foolish to think that the views that I enjoy from the platform of my work are views that my customers would ever want to block themselves from, and I'd be even more of a fool to think that these people would get something installed to accommodate little old me, as I hang from my cables outside of their homes.

Some of the time, I see things that I'd rather not see, but these are not necessarily things that I need to tell someone about. I guess you could consider me a 'mandatory reporter', inasmuch as my company has informed me and my fellow employees that, "if we see something, we should say something." I work for Skyclimbers, which is one of the premier window washing companies in all of San Diego. If you happen to be in need of our services, for your particular high-rise, please visit our website at skyclimberswindowcleaning.com. We do excellent work. And tell them that Daniel Voit sent you.

And, as an added bonus, we'll tattle on you if you're doing bad stuff in your place.

I tend to see things like middle-age balding white guys watching football in their fruit-of-the-looms, or overweight ladies trying to recapture their figures by poorly imitating the aerobic routines playing on their television screens. And, it's not like we are showing up unannounced — our scheduled appointments, whether we're washing at the Spire San Diego, or at the Manchester Grand Hyatt Hotel, or at the

Pacific Gate, are made known to the homeowners far enough in advance for them to be able to make plans to not be lounging in their skivvies at the time when their windows are set to be washed.

In those situations where I arrive to catch someone in the middle of something, it tends to go one of a couple different ways. The homeowner will notice me, and they'll stop what they're doing to keep me from getting a show. Or, they never end up noticing, which ends up being an awkward race for me to finish cleaning their windows as quickly as possible. If you've ever washed a window before (and who hasn't?), you know how hard it can be to focus on the glass that you're supposed to be cleaning, when something else is going on beyond the glass.

In all the years that I've been doing this, though, there's only been one time when I saw something that I ended up reporting. In fact, it was so disturbing that I called 9-1-1 right from the platform, as I was staring in on the scene. I even ended up being called as a witness, a few months later, during the criminal trial of the person responsible. In fact, with that trusty camera in my mind, I am still able to close my eyes and pull that picture up in perfect, high definition, color detail, just as if it were still before me.

It was a dining room area, with a gray-stained hardwood flooring. In the middle of the dining room floor was a long, steel and glass dining room table, with four chairs on each of its long sides and a chair at each of its ends — seating for ten. On the other side of the table from the windows that I was set to wash was the kitchen, all stainless steel appliances and high-end cabinetry. To my right, as I observed the tableau, was a seating area, on a lush carpet that would only exist in a home where the homeowner wasn't responsible for the cleaning of the carpets, all black leather sofas and overstuffed black leather chairs, huddled around what could only be described as a ridiculously large television.

And sadly, on the hardwood flooring, near to where the hardwood turned to the carpet of the living room area, lay a woman, quite obviously dead, for the size of the pool of blood that she was laying in and the pale, exsanguinated color of her skin. The blood had overflown the edge of the hardwood flooring, and had spilled into the carpeted area just a bit. The blood didn't look like fluid per se, but rather it looked like it had thickened to the point of being a bit congealed. The woman, in a cocktail dress of contrasting black and white geometric patterns, was looking out the windows at me with eyes that had glazed over to an extent that was morbidly horrifying.

I was glad not to have dropped my phone off of the side of that high rise, on that particular morning, I can tell you that.

Prompt Creation #230 - 2/12/21

"Whoa. Would you look at that!"

"I already was, my friend. I already was."

"What do you think the chances are that she's at an event like this without a plus-one?"

"Slim to none, dude."

"But still, what if? Right? What if she's here, all alone, and this is the night that she meets the love of her life, and what if that's me?"

"Now, now, hold on a minute. What if it's me? What if I'm the one that she's supposed to leave here with?"

They say that siblings make some of the closest friends. These two siblings, invited to this wedding reception by the groom, were as close as any two siblings/friends were ever likely to be. Because they were siblings, they shared a common base that was only to be found among siblings. After all, they say that blood is thicker than water. And yet, for these two, many of the family entrapments that make true sibling friendship a difficult thing to accomplish, didn't apply to them. Countless wedding receptions where the two of them have been in attendance, side by side. But –there's a first time for everything– never before had they both honed in on the same possible target, the same woman toward which to strive.

Patrick and Debbie were in a pickle, this time.

"What makes you even think you'd have a chance with a woman like that?"

"What's that supposed to mean?" Pat asked, feigning emotional injury. "I'm not qualified for 'girls like that'?"

"That's not what I meant and you know it. I'm just saying that there's something about
her that seems like it might be a bit out of your league."

"Oh yeah?"

"Yes, sir."
"Well, what about you? What makes you think that she's of the same persuasion as you? My gay-dar is pretty good, and I'm just not getting that impression from her."

Now it was Debbie's turn to pretend to be offended.

"Okay, first off — the entire homosexual community would appreciate it if uninformed heteroes would stop using the term 'gay-dar', thank you very much."

Pat chuckled. "Oops. My bad."

"And secondly," Debbie continued, "what makes you think that she's not the gal for me?"

Patrick thought for a moment, as he watched the woman who'd grabbed both his and his sister's attention. She was tall for a woman, about 5 – 10 or 5 – 11, in a strapless pink mini-dress and matching stiletto heels. She was thin, but not in an unhealthy way — rather, she seemed to have a glow of fitness. She was making her way to the head table, where Maryann and Michael were enjoying their wedding cake and champagne. The woman's shoulder length hair was the kind of blond that dared to be described as golden. She had a bounce in her step that suggested a confident joy, and Pat wanted to be by her side, later this evening, when she'd had enough of the festivities and decided to leave.

"Well???" Debbie elbowed her brother, demanding his logical argument against her candidacy.

"I know," he said to his sister. "We'll just go ahead and ask."

Pat was sitting on top of the bar stool, close enough to the bar to be able to lean back against the bar, beer bottle in one hand, to fish his phone out of his pants pocket with his other hand. He swiped on the screen to get into it, but then he waited. Debbie watched him as he was watching the mystery woman walking toward the front. The woman made her way around to the 'sitting side' of the long banquet table, approaching the newly-wed husband and wife. And, while it was Michael that first noticed the woman's approach, it was Maryann that stood and greeted her with a convivial hug, as they exchanged a few words, far beyond the earshot of the siblings seated at the bar.

As the mystery woman started to walk back to her seat, Patrick formed a text message to Michael and sent it off. He and Debbie watched as Michael noticed his phone, vibrating on the table in front of him. He grabbed it, read whatever Patrick had texted, smiled, and then looked over at the two of them, enjoying their libations at the bar. Debbie even raised her bottle of Bud in the air in a toast to him. Michael typed something into his phone, presumably sent it back to Pat, and set it back down on the table.

"What did you text him?"

"I asked him who she is."

Just then, the return text came in to Pat's phone with a little chirp.

"And?"

Patrick read the text aloud. "Cousin of Maryann's."

"Oh. That doesn't necessarily tell us anything in particular, does it?" Debbie asked her brother.

"Not really."

It was just about then that the woman in the pink mini-dress was arriving back at her seat, at a table that was far enough away from the head table to suggest that it was likely to belong to distant family members or former childhood friends or some other group of people, less important than those who would have garnered closer seats to the head table or to the buffet. On the contrary, Pat and Debbie had given up their seats at a table just two tables from Michael and Maryann, preferring to sit in a spot where the return trip to the bar was less of a chore. Since Michael and Patrick were coworkers at the same law firm, and former college lacrosse teammates, and since Michael was the last male that Debbie had ever dated, the two of them had landed some primo seats.

Debbie noticed that Maryann's cousin was easily the youngest person at her table, by a matter of decades, and that she was sitting alone in the way that a person can be sitting next to several people but can also obviously be of no association with them.

"I'm fairly certain that she didn't bring a date, Pat. There's no one at her table who might fit the bill."

"Very interesting." Pat replied, in his best impression of a detective on the case. Pat had never been any good at impressions.

And so, they sat like that for about twenty minutes, neither one of them deciding to pursue the conversation down that road. They drank their beers — Budweiser for Debbie and Miller Lite for Pat. They enjoyed each other's company, and the festive nature of the occasion, and especially the music that the DJ was playing –this guy was good– and they were happy to continue doing so. But then, Maryann's cousin in the pink mini-dress made her way to the bar, presumably to order a drink. She came up to the bar on Debbie's side, just a few feet down, and the bartender took her order for a vodka-and-tonic. A moment later, she was on her way back to her table over in the boondocks.

"Vodka-and-tonic." Debbie said, leaning over to Pat to allow for her to speak in a somewhat hushed tone.

"Really?"

"Yep. Just happened to overhear. What do you make of that?"

"Not my kind of a girl."

"Really? Why not? Half-hour ago, you were ready to buy her a drink and sing her a song."

Pat smiled at his sister's Tom Petty reference. She was good for things like that, good for a lot of things.

"Never could abide by the vodka girls. Something not right about them. Dated one in college. She always seemed to have something to prove."

"I see."

It was at that point that the cha-cha slide came on over the speakers near the dance floor. Michael and Maryann, and just about everyone else capable of dancing without displacing a hip joint, got up and headed out to the dance floor. Patrick and Debbie joined them all, and together, they danced the night away.

Prompt Creation #242 - 2/10/21

Richard "Bud" Robleski was one happy pig farmer. He couldn't remember the last stretch he'd had with so many sows and so many healthy litters of piglets, and –since it was still so early in the spring– there was a good chance that most of those sows would come into heat again with plenty of time for them to farrow a second time before year's end. At this rate it was going to be a banner year for his farm, and he couldn't have been any happier. Sitting on his front porch swing, which faced west –into the setting sun– Bud had the happy fatigue that can only come from a hard day's work, from knowing that you've done your best to make things successful. Physical labor is its own reward, were you to ask Richard Robleski, who was probably one of the most physically fit thirty-eight-year-olds in all of Knox County. But, it's also hard to argue with the results that one can achieve when one is dedicated to hard work and their dreams.

Bangor Springs was not likely to have a more eligible bachelor, among the 'plow-and-barn scene', than Bud Robleski –> Bud's farm had doubled in its financial assets every three years or so, ever since he'd come home from cow college, as his father put it. Bud Robleski had graduated near the top of his class at Michigan State University with a bachelor's degree in agribusiness management, and had been doing well for himself ever since.

He was living the dream, as it were.

But, he was also sitting on that porch swing alone.

Which, as things turned out, was probably for the best.

The porch swing faced to the west, and the sun setting behind the trees at the back side of the forty-three acres of soybean field across the street from his place was as picturesque as it could be. That soybean field belonged to Lloyd Stuckey, another one of the fine farmers in the Bangor Springs area, and the field was at that place of progress −not too long after planting− where it was just starting to show some green. As tens of thousands of tiny soybean plants were all just starting to poke out of the ground, making the rich soil appear from afar as if it were starting to grow a luscious green fur, Bud was enjoying watching the final rays of sunlight landing on that greenery, thinking to himself that this was most certainly what God had in mind when he created the crops of the fields.

And that was when he heard it.
A dull roar, almost imperceptible at first, coming from all directions and also from no particular direction, and growing louder by the second.

By the time Bud realized that the noise was coming from the east, from the other side of his house from where he was, there wasn't much time to do anything but watch.

It all ended up happening so fast, Bud didn't even really have time to register everything that was going on. The roar was getting louder and louder, and it seemed to be getting closer and closer to where he was. The old farmhouse window glass, very loosely held by its mortar in his old farmhouse window panes, started to shake and shudder with the volume of the approaching tumult. Of course, Bud was unable to see anything at all to the east, as he was positioned under his front porch, now standing in front of his front porch swing. So, in a single smooth motion of agility, Bud hopped the wrought iron fence on the front edge of the front porch, vaulting himself down and into the grass of his front yard. Three bounding leaps from there put him far enough in front of the house to be able to turn back around and look up into the sky.

Bud spotted the burning ball of fire, hurtling downward at a speed that boggled the young farmer's mind. It seemed obvious to him, by the trajectory of the thing, that it wasn't going to come down near to him at all. In the next half-second that passed before the fireball flew overhead, Bud was able to estimate that it was probably going to come down in the midst of the soybean field across the street –Merrifield Avenue– smack dab in the middle of Lloyd's brand new soybean field. And then, it was over him and past him and continuing onward, downward. Bud stared up into the sky at the thing –the burning thing– as it zoomed by and it couldn't have been more than a hundred feet in the air at that point. The quickest of glimpses that he was able to grab with his eye –in that split-second moment– captured three important pieces of information that Bud ended up processing with his mind only later.

The burning center of the ball of fire appeared to be a ship, an aircraft of some kind.

The speed of that ball of fire's travel was even greater than Bud had been able to estimate until it was directly overhead.

There was some sort of debris coming away –falling off– from the ship as it flew its final few hundred yards.

Then, as quickly as the whole hullabaloo had begun, it ended as the thing crashed into Lloyd Stuckey's beautiful field of newly sprouting soybean plants. The way that the crash happened, the amount of destruction that was wrought, was sure to have Lloyd fit to be tied when he found out about it. The roar of the descending fireball was replaced, at the moment of the crash, with an explosive boom that threatened to permanently deafen Knox County's most eligible pig farmer. Within a few moments of the crash, the debris that the aircraft had been shedding started making its way to the ground where Bud was standing. He felt it land on the shoulders of his shirt and on the top of the ball cap that he was wearing. It sprinkled onto him like fairy dust spilled by Tinkerbell herself.

It smelled like hot metal, like the smoke from a smelting kiln, all around. From above Bud, from across the street, as an easterly breeze blew the after-effects of the crash in his direction. He hadn't smelled that smell since the metal sculpture class he'd taken as an elective in college, almost two decades previous. Bud did his best to try to look across the street, to see what he could see from a distance. What Bud saw was a mess; a mess of dirt and torn up seedling soybean plants, and a mess of metal wreckage and destruction. The sun, as if deeply saddened by this whole unfortunate turn of events, decided not to tarry any longer in fleeing the scene altogether — it ducked behind the trees at the western edge of Lloyd's field. This set the whole field, with its leveled ruination, into a twilight dimness that made it even harder for Bud to make out any of the visual details at all.

And, had Bud Robleski been romantically involved with someone, had he been married or engaged or even just seriously seeing someone, there's a pretty gosh-darn good chance that he wouldn't have been on that porch swing alone. That he wouldn't have crossed Merrifield Avenue alone.

That he wouldn't have made his way into Lloyd's soybean field alone. Because he was a bachelor –thanks be to God– he wandered toward the epicenter of the crash site by himself.

Never to be seen or heard from again.

Prompt Creation #192 - 2/8/21

Chicago Metro Police have arrested him sixteen times in the past year, which hasn't been a problem for them —they were looking to arrest someone for something— and it hasn't been a problem for him, either. You see, Barney Moss really doesn't have much to do with his time, so spending that time in the jail cells of the precinct police department is just as good a place to spend the time as any, especially if the weather outside is inclement. The charge, each time, has been a preliminary charge of disorderly conduct, which isn't totally appropriate, since Barney's behavior is hardly ever disorderly. And yet, that's what the police claim when they contact the prosecutor's office. And, wonder of wonders, the prosecutor's office tells the police officers —every single time— to cut Barney loose, so he can go about his life.

They tend to pick him up on South Princeton Avenue, in Fuller Park, between 42nd Street and 51st.

The police who continue to pick him up only do so when what he tends to do with his time gets in the way of what other people are trying to do, what other productive people are trying to do. For, that's how it normally goes with people like Barney; the good people of the world don't have any problems with the existence of people like Barney, as long as they don't get in the way, or cause too much difficulty. The moderately self-impressed people of the world even make attempts to help people like Barney, from time to time, on their own terms and only to such an extent that such generosity doesn't really cost them anything.

Barney is best off when he is able to keep himself under his own control. "Don't step outside of the cage that the world is comfortable with you being in, Barney, and things will be just fine." He understands that he can't obstruct the flow of foot traffic, even though there isn't much foot traffic to speak of in Fuller Park, where Barney tends to do what he does. People walking in Barney's neighborhood should have known better. And while the occasional pedestrian might be somewhat obstructed by Barney's larger creations, normally –between his own ability to keep things under a tight rein and the absence of passers-by in Fuller Park– Barney is able to keep from getting in trouble.

He works out of an abandoned dumpster, in an alley that runs-north-south behind the homes on Princeton Avenue and Wells Street, in the 4200 block. Barney knows that the dumpster is abandoned because it doesn't have any of the insignia on its sides that would suggest that it belongs to some disposal company –say, Chicago Disposal, for example. Barney also 'staked out' the dumpster at first. He put some actual garbage in the dumpster, early last year, just to see if it was ever getting emptied. When he discovered that it wasn't ever getting emptied, Barney made the dumpster his own. He keeps all of his most important possessions in that dumpster. Coincidentally, it's actual garbage that Barney keeps in the garbage dumpster.

For you see, Barney is a sculptor. But, while some sculptors sculpt in clay or steel or marble, Barney makes sculptures out of garbage. And, as unappealing as this might sound, especially if you are the kind of person who prefers to be somewhat removed from your trash once you've decided in your mind that your detritus is just that –trash– then it might come to surprise you that the sculptures that Barney makes are actually quite beautiful. He uses the garbage that he keeps in the dumpster, and he's able to form it into 'statues' that dazzle everyone who gets to see them.

Not that many people ever do.

Prompt Creation #228 - 2/3/21

Long before the HIBS –or, the Holiday Inn, Bangor Springs– became the premier lodging destination for anyone who happened to be looking for a place to stay in south-central Knox County, Mr. Donald Antisdale was the sole owner and proprietor of a simple, if not somewhat dilapidated, motel out by the highway. It was a motel that barely made ends meet, back in the old days, because there really wasn't that much of a need for a premier lodging destination –or for even a mediocre lodging destination– outside of Bangor Springs. The HIBS, in more modern times, was able to be moderately more successful primarily because of the other businesses that had sprung up in the area in between Bangor Springs and Chester, especially those in the vicinity of the same highway (M-192) that Donald's motel had always catered to.

Back when the place was simply called The Bangor Springs Motel, Donald employed an employee or two, here and there, to help with the work that always seemed to pile up, usually because he wasn't quite fast enough to be able to stay on top of some of the things. The work that always got the better of Mr. Antisdale, the work that he avoided –usually by doing other things around the motel, some that needed doing and others that maybe didn't– was the maid work. While Donald was capable of changing the sheets on a bed, or emptying a motel room garbage can, keeping the place neat enough to avoid getting shut down for health code violations was beyond him.

While he would hire this maid, who might work at the motel for six months before moving on, or that maid, who might be a decent employee for all of a couple of weeks, the best maid he'd ever hired, in all of his years running the motel, and even in the years after he became a Holiday Inn franchisee, had been Karen Brooks. Karen was a meticulous person, probably the most meticulous person that Donald had ever known. She noticed things that no one else ever saw — the ring of dust on the top of the lampshade on the lamp, the crumbs that got caught between the wall and the desk that you had up against that wall, the lint and hair that would congregate around the pad at the bottom of the bed frame leg — Karen noticed it all, and in her noticing, she cleaned it all.

This was even more stunning when you considered Karen's particular situation.

She only had one arm.

Going all the way back in his memory, to the morning that she'd come into the motel front office, looking for work, Donald could remember being somewhat amused that a one-armed woman would show up, asking to be hired as a maid in a motel. The fact that she seemed to have one hundred percent confidence that she could do the job –that she exuded a self-assurance that didn't seem to correlate with her disability– was the primary reason that Donald had decided to hire her.

"I just don't get it, Ms. Brooks. How is it that you are going to be able to do what this job will require you to do, in light of your predicament?"

"Mr. Antisdale, what you see when you look at me isn't disability, it's inability. You're assuming that I can't do what you are going to need me to do because, in your mind, I shouldn't be able to do it. But, to be completely honest, you have no idea what I can or can't do. You're just jumping to conclusions."

Donald laughed, to have been so accurately summed up by this total stranger, who seemed to understand more about him after fifteen minutes of conversation than his wife, Laura, had understood about him during their first five years of marriage.

"In the end, it's probably going to be no skin off of my nose to give you a shot. I don't have a maid now, and I haven't had any prospects since the last maid left three weeks ago. Whether you can do the job or not, just letting you try to do the job is liable to end me up in a better place than I'm at right now."

"So, I'll start tomorrow. And, for the first month, you can pay me half of what you would've paid any other new maid under your employment."

"Now why would I do that?"

"Because," Karen Brooks said, "I need a place to stay."

And so, that's how it was. For the first month, Karen cleaned the motel during the regular business hours of the day, and she stayed in the motel room furthest from the main office –all the way down at the end– during her off-hours. During that first month, Donald's motel probably had only had about a dozen guests, but Karen had been busy the whole time — which wasn't to say that it took her very long to get much done. Rather, Karen had made it her project to be cleaning the uninhabited rooms with a highly thorough approach that would have nigh been impossible were there people checking in and out of those rooms. By working around the customers that were occasionally coming and going, she was able to keep up with their needs while also deep cleaning the rooms that were vacant.

When she first started doing this, after she'd finished her first 'top-to-bottom', as she called them, Donald checked on the work that she'd done, work that had taken her three full business days in a single motel room. He was absolutely floored to discover that he'd never seen the rooms so clean. He couldn't remember the place being as clean when the motel was first built, back in '58. She'd cleaned everything, as nearly as he could tell — EVERYTHING. In fact, standing in the midst of that first, immaculate room, looking around at the sparkle that the room seemed to have — on every surface, in every corner, in all of the nooks and crannies– Donald wondered how it was that she'd been able to do so much in just three days.

And, in about a month's time, she'd saved enough of her 'half-pay' to put a security deposit down on an apartment in Bangor Springs proper. At the time, Donald offered to let her continue to stay at the motel, free of charge even, mostly because it was nice having her around, in the event of a housekeeping emergency. Karen refused, but her moving away had no effect on the level of her effectiveness. For just shy of ten years, Donald's secret weapon in turning a first-time guest into a repeating guest was Karen Brooks. If he'd had a dollar for every time that someone told him that they'd never stayed in a motel so clean, he could have paid Karen what she was really worth to him.

And all of that with just one arm.

Prompt Creation #146 - 2/1/21

"I think our waitress is interested in you."

"What? What are you talking about?"

"Well, I've noticed that she's refilled your coffee six times."

"Okay?!?! Is this not proper? Should she *not* regularly be filling my coffee?"

"Paul, she's come over to refill your coffee after you've taken only a sip or two. She seems to be fixated on you."

Paul looked at Bruce, with some amount of confusion and mistrust on his face. The two of them, friends for almost three decades, knew each other well enough to be able to read the expressions on each other's faces pretty reliably.

"I think he's right, Paul. She has been over here quite a bit, and –in case you haven't noticed– she's not checking on our coffee."

Paul looked at Michael Hodge, not necessarily appreciative of him having teamed up with Bruce, to outnumber him on the subject. Then, Paul checked Bruce's coffee mug and Michael's — both of them were close to bone-dry. He looked back at his, to find it as full as was conceivably possible, without creating a spilling hazard. He looked up and quickly scanned the dining room of the Hilltop restaurant, found their waitress — standing behind the counter, who just so happened to be looking right back at him. Their eyes met, but then –in awkwardness and embarrassment– they both looked away.

"She's looking right at me, or at least she was, just now."

"See? I told you." Bruce was proud to be seemingly proven correct.

Bruce and Paul had been meeting for breakfast at the Hilltop, every other Tuesday, ever since Bruce got back from active deployment overseas. They invited Michael Hodge to join them for these breakfasts a few years back, as Michael was an up-and-coming businessman in the community, taking over for his father at the local hardware store, down on the corner of Front Street and Merrifield Avenue in Bangor Springs. The three of them got along pretty well, and their friendship was trusting and amiable.

"Here she comes again."

Paul turned, and spotted the waitress on her way over to the table, coffee pot in hand and a smile that seemed slightly larger than what you would have expected on her face.

"Refill?"

Paul looked down at his coffee mug, still so full as to make it impractical for anyone to try to refill it, and chuckled. The chuckle, and his attention on his mug, caught her attention, and she giggled in response. The maladroit nature of what was going on was just south of unbearable for Michael and Bruce, so Bruce broke the tension.

"Mike and I could use refills, if you wouldn't mind."

The waitress, whose name was Juliette –if you could believe that she was wearing the correct name tag– looked at the empty mugs of the two other men, and her face flushed with fright.

"I have to apologize. I don't know where my mind is this morning."

"I do." Michael mumbled, only slightly under his breath.

Juliette leaned over the table, standing in between Paul and Bruce, to fill first Mike's, and then Bruce's, coffee mugs. She was graceful and fluent in her motions as a waitress. Although Paul couldn't recall seeing her in the restaurant before this morning, she obviously had experience as a waitress from somewhere. Once she was finished, she asked if any of them needed anything, and then she left.

"Dude!" Bruce said, slapping Paul in the arm to make sure that he had his attention. "Did you see her nametag? Her name's Juliette. Maybe, you could be her 'Romeo'."

Bruce leaned back, pleased with how witty he'd sounded, and Paul gave Bruce the look that he always gave Bruce when he would try to be witty and end up failing.

"Dude," Paul slapped Bruce in the arm –as payback– "that's not how Romeo's 'Juliet' spelled her name."

"Well, it's not like I would know." Bruce defended himself. "Shakespeare and I don't exactly have a close relationship."

Michael chimed in. "Technically, you could make the argument that Juliet probably never spelled her name either way, since very few people, on average, would have known how to write in the thirteenth century."

"However, considering that she was most likely a member of the Italian upper-class…"

And that's how the three of them spent the next half-hour or so — bantering back and forth about this thing and that. Just passing some friendly time together. During that time, Juliette had been sure to make sure that none of them ran out of coffee. When she came to the table a final time, Paul decided to wrap up the morning fun.

"I think I'm ready for my check."

"Me, too." Michael added.

"Me, three." said Bruce.

"You act like you're three." Michael said to Bruce.

"And you speak like you're three." From Paul. "So monosyllabic."

"I don't know why I put up with this kind of abuse. I can't be this hard up for companionship."

"I'll go finish your checks." Juliette said, and she was gone.

"Seriously, Pauley," Bruce said, leaning over to be able to speak in a hushed tone,
"you've got to get her phone number or something."

"Perhaps, I will."

Each of the men made their way to the counter to pay, which was the custom at the Hilltop. Juliette rang out Michael, and then Bruce, and then Paul.

As Paul's receipt finished printing out of the cash register, Juliette ripped it off, set it on the counter to write something on it, and then handed it to Paul. As the three of them left the building to head to their individual vehicles, Paul read what Juliette had written at the bottom of his receipt.

"So," Bruce butted in, "what are you reading on that receipt there? Seems to have you enraptured."

"See for yourself." Paul handed the receipt to Bruce and Michael, for them to see that Juliette had asked Paul to call her sometime, and had included her phone number in the note.

Prompt Creation #127 - 1/29/21

Darlene Roberts honestly didn't know how it was that she was able to do what she was doing.

After all, she'd never been to Hong Kong, never even been to China. Her understanding of international business practices was non-existent, so it was a mystery to her why she'd even been asked by the Vice-President of Production to accompany him on a fact-finding trip to the heartland of the company's fiercest competitor. Two weeks ago, when she told her best friend and fellow coworker Julia about being invited to go on the trip, Julia said, "He probably invited you to go because your butt looks nicer than his wife's."

The most surprising part, by far however, had turned out to be her ability to speak in perfect Cantonese upon her arrival.

She was so good at it that her business hosts at Huntawei Global Products were in awe of her grasp of the language, including its most subtle nuances. They told her as much, and she understood not only their comments, but also the bigotry against Westerners that was the sub-text of their amazement. They asked her how she came to know the language, this skinny blond white lady from Tulsa, Oklahoma, and Darlene didn't even have an answer to give them.

And of course, Mr. Henderson was in awe.

"I never knew that you spoke Cantonese!"

"Would it surprise you to learn that I didn't know that I could, either!'

"Ha! And you're so funny, too! You must come with me on all my China trips in the future."

All joking aside, the process of doing it, of exhibiting an intellectual skill that you didn't know that you had, was a sensation that she couldn't remember ever experiencing before. Most of the things that a person does, they do from the experience of having done it before. Your performance is mostly a memory, your efficiency a measure of your previous efficacy. But, to do something that you didn't know that you could do was totally different; it was like information was being pulled –dragged– out of a recess in her mind by other administrative functions of her brain, functions that were aware of something in the recesses that she wasn't consciously acquainted with.

And, she must have learned it from somewhere, right?

The business trip was a huge success, and Sooner Industries had landed a major cooperation agreement with Huntawei Global Products; Mr.

Henderson told Darlene four or five times during the final dinner in Hong Kong –which ended up being more of a marathon celebration between the hosts and the guests that only started out as dinner and ended up several hours later in a bar in Mongkok, where Darlene learned what baijiu was– that he believed that the trip had been such a success mostly because of the impression that Darlene had had on their business hosts.

For Darlene, however, the trip had been a largely negative experience. It was jarring to try to come to terms with something like this — she didn't really know how to handle what she'd learned about herself. She didn't have any reason to expect that she'd been to Hong Kong or China as a child. Darlene's mother had been a cocktail waitress in Muskogee for most of her life, that was before she died from lung cancer at the ripe old age of fifty-five, a couple of years back. Darlene's father had been killed in an oil drilling accident when she was barely out of diapers. All that Darlene could remember of her thirty-seven years of life, she'd never been outside of the Plains states, except for that one trip she took, during the summer after she graduated from high school, with two of her closest high school pals, down to San Diego.

She just couldn't figure where she'd picked up an Oriental language that she'd been previously unaware of.

And, if she'd not picked it up from somewhere –if there wasn't a legitimate theory to explain how she'd done this thing that she didn't know that she could do– then all that remained were the crackpot theories.

Maybe she had a brain tumor. Maybe she'd been Chinese in a previous life. Maybe she was an international spy with amnesia who'd actually spent a lot of time in a place that she had no recollection of. Maybe the drinking water in her neighborhood –McClure Park– had more in it than just trace amounts of fluoride.

Maybe she'd been abducted by aliens and they'd planted Cantonese in her head, like downloading an ebook to a tablet.

While none of these answers felt like they were the right one, Darlene felt more and more uneasy about the possibility that she might not be able to discover the answer. How does one explain having an ability that one ought not to have? Maybe, she could start seeing a psychotherapist who'd be able to suggest the possible ways –the real, possible ways– that she could be able to do what she ought not to be able to do.

And these questions just led to other questions. Could she speak Mandarin or Hunanese, in addition to Cantonese? Did she have any relatives, near or distant, with ties to China? What other languages might she know and not even know about it?

As Darlene looked out the window of the plane, making its way back to the North American continent, she stared down at as much Pacific Ocean as one could soak up with one's eyes. All the while, staring down at nothing but water, she was really regretting having said 'Yes' to coming on this business trip.

Prompt Creation #212 - 1/27/21

It felt wrong to him, every time it happened, even though he knew, deep down inside, that he'd done nothing wrong. It wasn't as if Matt was even in control of what was happening. So, why should there be any guilt?

And yet, there was. Every time.

This morning was the sixth time.

The previous five times, the picture became clearer, each time. The definition in the details became more perspicuous, as if the fog was clearing, each time. He saw the first time as if through a thick fog. The second time — through a less thick fog, and so on. Having woken now from the sixth occurrence, things were starting to take on the clarity of a 4K Ultra television broadcast. He didn't know whether or not, when this happened to other people –this certainly had to have happened to someone else, at some other point in human history, right?– if this was how it worked: the lucidity growing and growing. Whether or not anyone else had experienced this before, Matt was experiencing it now, had been experiencing it for the last couple of months, and the experience seemed as if it was swelling toward something, inching toward an eventuality of some kind.

Each time, he woke up, next to a woman who was not the woman that he'd been dreaming of.

Each time, he woke up next to his wife of eleven years. The two women, different in how solidly each of them were connected to him —one as solidly as could be, and the other not solidly at all— were different in almost every other way, as well. His wife was tall, slightly taller than him, and blond. The woman in his dreams was slight and small and brunette of an auburn hue. His wife was very solidly built —she always joked about being big-boned— but the woman in his dreams seemed almost elfin in her stature, as if the next strong breeze would whisk her away.

Matt was sure —absolutely positive— that he'd never seen this woman who'd now appeared in his dreams a half-dozen times. Not at his work, for sure. He was an investment banker with the largest firm in the Midwest, and all of the women that worked in Matt's office were at least somewhat familiar to him. He was sure that he'd not seen this woman at his gym, where he tried to hit the weights or to pound out a couple of miles on the indoor track at least three times a week. He was sure that he'd not seen her where he normally shopped for this thing or that.

Matt was convinced that she wasn't a real person; at least, not a real person with whom he was acquainted.

He'd asked his favorite coworker –Jim– whether or not he'd ever dreamed of a woman that he didn't know, to which Jim replied, "Only two or three times a week, my friend. Not all of us are lucky enough to have married the prom queen." Matt asked a couple of his buddies from the bar where he liked to grab a beer after work, but he got the same types of responses from them that he got from Jim at work.

If this kind of thing happened to other guys, those other guys weren't talking about it with their friends, apparently.

Matt couldn't remember it having happened on a Friday night/Saturday morning before. As he laid in bed, waiting for his wife to wake, without any particular place to be, he was working himself into a bother. What if this never stopped? What if he continued to dream about this mystery woman for the next year? The next ten years? Until he died? Did the fact that he was dreaming about another woman signify something about his psyche? About his level of subconscious devotion to his wife? Shouldn't he be dreaming of his wife? If he's bound to be dreaming of some woman, shouldn't it be her?

And then, as if stirred by the activity of his mind, his wife rolled over in the bed next to him, turning to face him. She sleepily opened her eyes and they made contact with his.

"Mornin', sleepy head."

"Good morning, Matty."

"How did you sleep?"

"Every night I wake up next to you was a good night's sleep, my main man."

They laid next to each other, just gazing at each other, for a moment or two.

"Hey, Matty. I've been thinking. Why don't we try that new donut shop that just opened up over on Alexander Ave.?"

"That's a grand idea." Matt replied.
And just like that, they were up and out of bed, with visions of long johns and fritters in their heads. They each threw on a presentable set of active wear and were out the door in fifteen minutes, give or take.

'Glazed and Confused' had only been open on Alexander Avenue, between 5th and 6th Street, for a matter of days. As close as it was to their home, Matt and his wife were likely to be regular customers, if they turned out to be any good. Once inside the front door, his wife turned to him and said, "You know what I like; I'm going to grab a table." as she headed off in a different direction.

Matt, at the front counter, spent a minute or two, perusing what was available under the glass of the display. When he'd found the raspberry filled donut that he knew his wife would want, and the custard-filled long john that his own general practitioner would have frowned upon, Matt stood up straight, to get someone's attention.

A short, slight brunette made her way to the front to assist him.

Prompt Creation #31 - 1/25/21

Carlos meant the world to her, which she hardly would've imagined was possible a year ago.

Carlos's father, on the other hand, he was a non-entity. She'd never even known his name, as unfortunate as that was. It was the classic story. Girl has too much to drink at a party. Makes a decidedly bad decision. Ends up reaping what was sown, both figuratively and literally. You've heard it before, so there's no point in retelling it.

This story is different, though, for a couple of different reasons, the first of which being that Summer decided –after getting the confirmation of her pregnancy– that she was going to keep the child.

On a conscious level, Summer was looking for someone to love, for someone to love her. A child, dependent on her and capable of being the object of her affections, would do just fine. Subconsciously, though, Summer suffered from a strikingly low level of self-esteem, and the plan to become a mother would serve to bolster her ego, psychologically speaking.

The pregnancy was pretty normal, as far as pregnancies go. She had a good support system around her — her mother had been supportive of her decision, Summer's dad not so much, and she was receiving support from a local pregnancy care center in her community. Her friends, the few that she had, were being supportive as well, in the way that really good friends will often be. Without the support, making it through those nine months would've been pretty tough. As it was, it had been difficult, but not too much so.

Then, came the birth. It had been pretty taxing, going through it alone, but what else are you going to do? When the situation warrants a particular approach, that's what you do. It's not like Summer was going to get a hold of the baby's father, to have him by her side –a stranger holding her hand and helping her through the contractions. The hospital staff had been as helpful as they could be, and just like she did during the pregnancy itself, Summer made it through on the strength of her spirit.

Those first couple of days, in the hospital, Summer asked for help from every agent and agency that was available to her. You got used to doing that, when you were on your own, and Summer had learned –as a result of this whole experience– that it was often easier to ask for help from complete strangers than it was from people that you knew. So often, she'd gotten less help –and more condemnation and judgment– from the people that she knew, when she asked for help. The medical professionals in the hospital, and the social services agents working alongside those medical workers, they were willing to be helpful out of some intrinsic drive to be of assistance.

When she'd been discharged from the hospital, with Carlos in his car seat in the back of her car, she was confident that she'd be able to make it through this on her own.

She used the internet a lot, in the first couple of months, with Carlos at home, to answer questions that she had about this and that. What does diaper rash look like and how do you treat it? At what point should you be concerned with constipation in your infant? How to safely microwave formula? While she was trying to do her best, and while her support system was pretty decent, she was discovering that parenting a child was a massive undertaking.

And, in the first two months with Carlos, Summer had been in contact with the pediatrician to make sure that things were going as they should — as a new mother, she really didn't know what to expect. There was a well-baby check-up at one month that Summer and Carlos attended, just as they should. They were a couple of days late for the two-month check-up, but the secretaries in the pediatrician's office assured Summer that it wasn't that big of a deal, to be off by a couple of days.

With Carlos, everything seemed to be going according to the development timelines that Summer was reading about on her smartphone pretty much all of the time, at least when she wasn't doing things with Carlos. He was sleeping about as much as was normal for a newborn. His physical development was coming along. It all seemed fairly normal.

But then, about a week after the two-month well-baby check-up, Carlos started teething. Summer knew that this wasn't necessarily abnormal, but she called the pediatrician anyway. They confirmed that it wasn't peculiar, and they gave her advice about how to ease those first two bottom teeth through the gums.

But, it wasn't his bottom teeth that were coming in. It was the top teeth. And not the top front teeth, either. The canine cuspids. When Summer told the secretaries at the pediatrician's office about this, the pediatrician asked for Summer and Carlos to come in for a look-see.

During this look-see, the pediatrician asked Summer —once again— if she was sure that she couldn't provide any information at all about Carlos's father. To which Summer replied —once again— that she really didn't know anything about him at all. In the end, the pediatrician chalked it up to some kind of a genetic abnormality (on the father's side) that probably wasn't going to amount to much at all.

That diagnosis turned out to be very, very wrong.

Prompt Creation #100 - 1/22/21

"I just want to hug him. I know it's the wrong time, the wrong place, but I don't care."

"At this point, Maxine, I don't think it matters much, one way or the other, whether you do or you don't.

Maxine Smithers and her lawyer –Walter Tidey– were standing outside of his law office, as he'd offered to see her out to her pickup truck parked off of Front Street. They'd stopped, before making it quite to the vehicle, because Maxine had glanced down the sidewalk to the east, watching the man who'd been her husband as recently as fifteen minutes ago, the man that was now her ex-husband, walking away — presumably headed to the bar that he owned, only about a quarter-mile in that direction.

"Wait here a second, would ya', Mr. Tidey?"

Maxine didn't wait to hear whether or not Walter was going to wait for her there. Rather, she was running to catch up to Bruce, her first love, her high school sweetheart, but more recently, the bane of her existence. She ran past him, to come to a stop in front of him, as he was making his way to his bar. As he recognized her in front of him, blocking his path, he stopped. It was then that Maxine took him by surprise with the hug that she'd felt compelled to give him.

"I don't expect that hugging after signing your divorce papers is something that former couples tend to do." Bruce opined.

"I'll bet it happens more often than you might think." she countered.

"Perhaps you're right."

He seemed defeated to her, just then — conquered. He looked exhausted and vanquished and that was a look that she'd only rarely had the opportunity to see on the countenance of one Bruce Randolph. Maxine figured she'd probably been witness to that look more often than any other living soul. Just then, it struck her how often they disagreed during all of their conversations, how often they bantered and argued. It was truly a habit with them, and it was only now that Maxine was recognizing that debate was their colloquial norm. To hear him –now– agreeing with her, just to avoid a fight, was to hear something that she'd immediately recognized as a rarity.

The two of them stood, like that –just looking at each other– in front of the Bangor Springs Five and Dime, for what seemed like years. The five and dime was one of a handful of stores between the local lawyer's office and the place where Bruce slung beers and cocktails most nights. It felt like the end of something, and while some people shoot out of a theater at the end of a movie, others watch the credits roll, not wanting it all to have ended.

"I think I'm going to head out of town. Get a new start. Somewhere away from here." Maxine said, breaking the tense silence between them.

"You don't have to do that on my account, Max. I wouldn't mind if you stayed around."

"I know, Buck. It's not that I feel like I need to leave. I feel like I want to leave. I've been thinking about the southwest, maybe western Texas, or New Mexico, maybe even Arizona."

Bruce seemed to think for a minute, standing in front of his ex-wife. Maxine could tell that he was weighing his words, weighing the importance they would have in how she'd hear them.

"Maxine, I've always wanted you to be happy. I'm sorry that you couldn't be happy with me. I remember, not so long ago, when you were happy with me, when we were happy together. But, if being divorced from me is going to make you happy, if being divorced from me –on the other side of the country– is going to make you happy, I guess at this point, I'll take whatever you're willing to give me."

Maxine didn't know how to respond to that, didn't know if there was a way to respond to what he'd said. She suspected that any response would be improper. So, rather than soil this, his last expression of his affection for her, she simply smiled and turned slightly to walk away, past him and back in the direction from which she'd come.

"Take care of yourself, Bruce. Goodbye."

And she committed to walking away. One foot in front of the other, left then right then left again, stride after stride leading her away from him, away from 'them', away from what she'd always known.

Away from what had failed.

She knew that he was probably watching her go, and she knew that if she stopped, and turned back toward him, that it would ruin her escape velocity — the speed that she was going to need to be able to get clear of this whole thing. Her momentum grew, and she felt the gravity that would have pulled her back into him, back into 'them', growing weaker and weaker. The closer she got to the front of the office of Mr. Walter Tidey, Esq. –who had decided to stand guard, waiting for her, she could see as she got within range– the more Maxine wondered if Bruce would still be standing where he was, in front of the five and dime, when she got there.

But he wasn't. As she arrived in front of her lawyer, next to her pickup, she turned to look back to the east, and Bruce was nowhere to be seen. Presumably, he'd completed his trek to the bar, gone inside.

And that was fine.

"Thanks for waiting, Mr. Tidey."

"Don't mention it, kid. My next appointment's not for a few minutes yet."

Maxine looked back again, to the east, and of course Bruce was still not there. She reached out her hand, offering it to her lawyer in gratitude for his services, and after the handshake, she made her way around to the driver's side of her truck and got inside. She purposefully headed west in the truck, not wanting –at that particular moment– to lose any ground to the east.

Prompt Creation #213 - 1/20/21

"Well, my goodness. Dr. Antisdale, what has you out on a Friday night, doing fifteen miles over the posted speed limit for this area?"

It wasn't that Officer Andrew Billings was surprised to have pulled over such a big fish; if you work long enough in the same town, you end up catching all kinds of people from that town, in all kinds of compromising positions. Rather, Billings was curious as to what would have the town's only practicing G.P. in the area of that town at a time of night that was most certainly not business hours. Billings knew that Roland Antisdale was not from Bangor Springs, just as he himself was not. And, while they shared that in common, Billings was pretty sure that only one of them was 'on the clock'.

He was pretty curious as to what brought the doctor into a residential neighborhood in town, to hot-rod all over the place.

"Hello, Officer…"

"Billings, sir. Officer Andrew Billings."

"Of course. Now I remember. Good evening, Officer."

Andrew had enough experience as a police officer to be able to tell the difference between all manner of different reactions to being pulled over. You have the people who play it calm and cool to try to get brownie points for playing it calm and cool — they're not ever really quite fully capable of pulling off the whole 'calm and cool' vibe. Then, there's the actual calm and cool people, who realize that it's not worth getting all emotional over a traffic ticket, especially if you were guilty in the first place. Then –the opposite of the calm and cool folk– you've got the 'over-the-toppers' who just jump off the deep end when you pull them over.

Lots of different possible reactions that people have, even more than those listed above, Officer Billings knew. But, the one that you needed to always be keen to, the one that you always needed to be on the lookout for, was the 'guiltier-yet' suspect. The thing about a 'guiltier-yet' traffic ticket was that they were hiding something.

Dr. Antisdale was hiding something, and Billings knew it almost immediately. He could tell by the look in the doctor's eyes.

"So, Dr. Antisdale. You don't live in this town. It's Friday night. 9:53 p.m.. Your office hours ended about five hours ago. So? What are you doing here?"

Officer Billings knew that Dr. Antisdale lived in Benton Harbor, which is in the north end of Knox County. Bangor Springs is just a half-dozen miles north of the Indiana border with Michigan, which would be decidedly south-county.

"Look, Officer Billings. I don't mean to be rude, but if you're going to issue me a ticket, I'd prefer that you just get on with it, rather than drawing the whole process out. I'm just a few minutes out from a meeting where I am expected to be, and I'd prefer not to be late, if it's all the same to you."

Andrew had learned during his police training that there was something suspicious about traffic stops where the suspect wanted to be out from under the gaze of the police officer as quickly as possible. Traffic stops tend to eclipse other concerns –while they're happening– so individuals who become avoidant of the attention from the police might actually have something grander –more illicit– than just violating traffic rules.

Dr. Antisdale was exhibiting the classic signs of being 'guiltier-yet'. As such, Andrew decided to escalate things.

"Dr. Antisdale, there is something about your demeanor this evening that is causing me to be a little concerned. Do you have any reason to object to a search of your vehicle?"

Andrew thought that it was unlikely that one guy could be capable of graduating from medical school but also incapable of understanding a scenario during which one might be giving away one's legal rights. Although it was a long shot, the cards had been played.

"Officer Billings, I've got nothing to be concerned about."

"Then," Andrew began, "please step out of the car and make your way to the front of the vehicle."

"Certainly, Officer."

Dr. Antisdale got out of his Mercedes, closing the door behind him, and made his way to the front of the vehicle. Andrew followed closely behind the doctor, all the way to the front hood.

"Now, Dr. Antisdale, please place the keys to the vehicle on the hood of the car."

Roland Antisdale did this without objection or debate. Andrew reached over and grabbed the key fob for the vehicle, locating on the fob the button for releasing the rear trunk lid. Andrew noticed that the audible click on the trunk of the vehicle caught Dr. Antisdale's attention.

And that's where he found it — Officer Billings found four boxes of prescription medication in the trunk of the Mercedes, all four boxes apparently full of oxycontin. Andrew did the quick math in his head. Each box contained forty cartons, and each of the cartons contained a dozen 60-mg pills. There were almost 2000 doses of opioid narcotic in the trunk of the doctor's car.

Andrew returned to the front of the vehicle, where the doctor was still silently waiting for it all to be over with.

"Well, doc. I'm not quite sure what to say about what I just found in the trunk of your car. While I try to think of something to say, why don't you place your hands behind your back, please?"

"Are you arresting me, Officer?"

"I most certainly am, Doctor. You have about $150,000 worth of drugs in the back of your car and you've yet to offer me a legitimate reason for them being there. I'd suggest you speak now or I'm going to be booking you at the Bangor Spring police department here in a few minutes."

Andrew looked at the doctor, half-expecting that he would offer some kind of lame excuse or cockamamie story to explain things away. Instead, Roland looked right into Andrew's eyes with a look of sincere gratitude.

"Honestly, Officer, I'm glad that you caught me. Chances are, I was going to keep doing this until someone stepped in to stop me."

"Doc, as much as I would love to hear your confession, I'm not your priest and it's not legally in your best interests to treat me as such. I'd suggest you use your cell phone, once we get back to my office, to call your lawyer — the two of you can figure out how you might divest yourself of the information that seems to be burdening you so."

Dr. Antisdale paused for a moment, still looking very cordially in the officer's direction, before saying…

"Still, Officer, I have to say thank you. Maybe now I'll be able to start my climb out of this hole."

Prompt Creation #104 - 1/18/21

"You smell terrible! What happened?"

Officer Mya Hopkins, the dispatcher for the department, never minced words, and the fact that she didn't had a tendency to get on people's nerves. Frank Moody, however, had become accustomed to it a long time ago, having worked with her for a number of years, and it was only in certain situations, where Frank was already a little on the edge, that Mya's brand of crass bluntness was more than he could bear.

"I don't want to talk about it, Mya. I'm going to grab some paperwork off of my desk, and then I'm going home. I will spend the rest of my shift there, working on that paperwork, unless anyone has any objections."

Officer Moody walked right past Mya's dispatch desk, almost without breaking stride, as he announced his plans for the rest of the day, the smell emanating from his clothes spread out behind him like a wake. Mya got up from her desk and followed after him, wanting to continue the discussion.

"Gee, I don't know Frank. Do you think that the chief would approve of that?"

He stopped and turned to face her, and it was then, as she closed the distance between her and Frank, that Mya discovered that the smell was much worse up close. The smell had a cloying thickness to it, but also an earthiness that reminded Mya of rotten vegetation. If the smell of rot and chocolate cake could be combined into some mad mutant smell, that was what Frank smelled like.

"I have no idea whether or not the chief would approve. But I do know that he's not here, and that he's not due back from Newburg until the end of the business day. As nearly as I can tell," Frank said, after a quick scan of the police department office, "I'm the ranking officer in the room right now."

Mya didn't take any offense at the statement, primarily because it wasn't very often that Frank Moody pulled rank on anyone, especially her, and additionally because she knew he did outrank her by about six months on the job. He must be particularly upset to be so forceful with her.

"Before you go, at least just tell me what happened."

Frank felt like Mya was probably one of the only women in the world who he'd ever had a problem saying 'no' to. A few years back, he'd thought about pursuing a romantic relationship with her, but he decided that it would've ended up being more trouble than it was worth, what with office politics and police procedure likely to get in the way. Currently, they shared a friendly, collegial relationship —which was probably for the best— but she still had a way of talking him down. Her voice whispered to his soul, somehow.

Frank sat in the chair behind his desk, and Mya sat in the chair normally reserved for those individuals with whom Frank was conducting official police business. It had been a slow day in the Bangor Springs police department, and there wasn't another soul in the office at the moment, no one to disapprove of the slight breach in etiquette.

"Well," Frank began, after a deep sigh, "it all started when you dispatched me over to the Stuckey farm on South Merrifield."

"Right," Mya remembered, "the report of crop destruction."

"Right. Except there wasn't any crop destruction. Lloyd's son, Chris, was out riding his quad —without his dad's permission— few days back and lost control of it. Ran it through the soybean field and then neglected to tell anyone about it. After five minutes of asking him some questions, he folded like a piece of paper. Lloyd grounded him for a month."

"So," Mya seemed confused, "what does any of that have to do with the stench rolling off of you in waves?"

Frank looked genuinely offended, and Mya was almost immediately sorry for being so insensitive to how uncomfortable he must be feeling. She thought of apologizing, but Frank started up again, apparently not that wounded.

"As I was heading back to my squad car, getting ready to radio back in to you, Old Man Hobbs pulled into Lloyd's driveway, right behind me."

"Blocking you in?"

"Yep. In that beat-up ol' Chevy pick-up of his. I still don't know how he keeps that thing running. It's held together by chicken wire and duct tape."

"So, what happened?" Mya asked.

"Well, he got out and came up to me and asked me to follow him out to his place."

"What?" Mya objected, "Out on Elcot Lane? That's half-way to Chester?!?!"
"I know it is. But, I could tell from the look on his face that it was serious. He told me that something was wrong with Dorothy."

Mya paused to reflect on the puzzle of Dorothy Hobbs. Mya –and most of Bangor Springs– had always figured that there was a special place in heaven reserved for anyone who could stand to put up with Warren Hobbs. Dorothy had a level of patience and grace that was unmatched in Knox County, and that made her the perfect wife for Old Man Hobbs.

Most of the other people in town couldn't even stand to be around the man.

"So, I followed him out to his place. I didn't radio it in because I wasn't necessarily sure what I was going to find when I got there. I didn't want to make it police official."

Mya knew what 'police official' was. Keeping certain parts of the job off of the public record –in the event that someone might have questions down the line– was a standard operating procedure.

"When I got there, he showed me in to see Dorothy, who was sitting in a lounger in the living room. She was as white as a sheet, and I could feel the heat on her before I even got close enough to check to see if she was breathing. I asked Warren what could have caused her to get ill, and he didn't know –at least not initially. So, I called for an ambulance from Chester to come and pick her up. And, wouldn't you know it, the old coot tried arguing with me about it."

"Figures." Mya chimed in.

"So, I distracted him by asking him some more questions about her illness. He said he couldn't think of anyone that they'd come in contact with who'd been sick, and he didn't know if they'd eaten anything strange. That was when it occurred to him."

"What?"

"He said, 'Maybe it was the new batch of carrot wine.'"

Mya gasped. The idea that Old Man Hobbs was making his own hooch hadn't crossed her mind, but it was the missing piece to the puzzle. The smell on Frank finally made sense. Anyone experienced with the fermentation process probably would have recognized the scent right off the bat, but Mya was ignorant of that whole realm.

"That's right," Frank continued, "he took me out to one of his barns, where he had his fermenters and his other wine-making supplies all set up. The place reeked to high heaven. I wonder if I'll ever be able to get this stench out of my clothes."

"But Frank, isn't that stuff all supposed to be a sealed process? It's not supposed to smell that bad, is it?"

"Mya, what I know about fermenting I could write on my pinky-nail in a twelve-point font. But I told Old Man Hobbs that he ought to be more careful. He's liable to fatally poison someone otherwise. That was about the point in time when the ambulance showed up. Warren rode in it, with his wife, off to Chester."

Mya sat back in the chair for a moment, thinking about all of the things that were going on in the lives of people all over this town, things that no one even knows anything about. Old Man Hobbs making carrot wine in his back barn had most certainly not been on her BINGO card when she woke up that morning.

"Frank," she said, with a smile on her face, "as the other acting officer on duty in this department here today, I formally agree that it would be best for you to leave this place before the smell drives me out of my mind."

"Smooth, Mya. Real smooth." Frank said as he grabbed the paperwork on his desk, got up, and walked out of the office.

Prompt Creation #133 - 1/15/21

"Darn it, Amy. Quit eating my pudding cups."

Darrell stood up straight and turned, so that he could face Amy and receive any reaction that was coming his way. He stood there, with the refrigerator wide open and the door in his right hand, practically daring her to say something to him.

Amy was initially speechless.

Chuck Harper leaned back in his chair, seated at the table in the middle of the teacher's lounge, excited to watch what was sure to be one of the most exciting things that he was going to see today. It wasn't that Chuck enjoyed his coworkers going at each other like cats and dogs, but he knew from experience that fights like these rarely amounted to much, and they were somewhat fun to watch, in a childish and voyeuristic kind of way. And, because Chuck had been a teacher for more than twenty-five years, he'd seen almost all of the 'fun' that a classroom had to offer. For some reason, though, interpersonal workplace drama just always got him going.

Chuck was sitting at the table with a smile on his face, as if a great treat was sitting on the table right in front of him. He wondered where his best friend

—and fellow veteran teacher— Miles Mitchell was, because it was going to be a shame if Miles missed these fireworks.

Amy began her counter-attack.

"What makes you think I'm the one who's eating them, Darrell? You got any proof?"

"I've got half a dozen people who've come to me to say that they've seen you in here, eating my pudding cups. Half a dozen people!"

Chuck wasn't aware of the root cause of the animosity between Amy and Darrell, but that was largely because he was such a veteran teacher, and this made him so old that the rest of the teachers found him distant and unrelatable. While it seemed to Chuck like many of the teachers that he worked with were perpetually in their mid-to-late twenties, he just kept getting older. This didn't really bother him —not that much, anyway— but it did make it harder and harder for him to downplay how excited he was that retirement was much closer for him than it was for any of them.

"There's no way you've got a half-dozen witnesses. What you've got is a half-dozen liars who are out to get me, just like you've been out to get me ever since I started working here."

"Well," Darrell replied, "I wouldn't be out to get you if you would just QUIT EATING MY PUDDING CUPS!"

While the rising volume level was making this more enjoyable, what Chuck really enjoyed seeing was how animated the two of them were getting. Amy and Darrell were probably –at this exact moment– completely incapable of understanding that they were arguing about Snack Packs. Chuck could remember, back in the day, when Snack Packs came in tiny metal cans, with peel-back metal lids. As Chuck tried to figure in his mind whether or not they'd stopped packaging Snack Packs in metal cans, before or after these two youngsters were born, the building principal walked in.

This worried Chuck, primarily because he thought there was a good chance that the principal would put the kibosh on this fight before it got a chance to really take off. That would be a shame.

"What in the name of Mike is going on in here?" Mrs. Charlotte Timmons asked. She was 'Char' to her friends, with a soft kind of an 'sh' consonant at the front. She was Principal Char to the students who disliked her the most, and this was pronounced with a hard 'ch' sound, so she ended up coming off like an arsonist or something. Everyone else just called her Mrs. Timmons.

"Mrs. Timmons, Darrell has accused me of stealing his food out of the staff refrigerator, and I was just trying to defend myself."

Darrell took the opportunity to chime in.

"And I was just explaining to Amy that I know that she's the one who's been eating my pudding cups because of the witnesses who've come to tell me all about it."

And just like that, they were back at each other, seemingly unconcerned with the fact that the principal was standing right in the doorway of the teacher's lounge, having come in to yell at the two of them, but completely incapable of getting a word in edgewise.

"There's no way you've got witnesses."

"Oh yeah?!?!"

"Yeah!"

"That's it!" Principal Timmons said, in a huff and a stomp of her fashionable three-inch heel. "Mr. Ross, report back to your classroom. Ms. Colburn, report to my office."

"But," Darrell started to object, "I haven't even had a chance to eat my lunch yet."

"Mr. Ross, go now!"

Darrell moped his way out of the teacher's lounge, out past Mrs. Timmons, followed by Amy, the two of them snipping snide comments at each other the whole way out. Darrell turned left out the door, to head back to his room, while Amy turned right to head to the principal's office, just down the hall.

This left the principal and Chuck Harper in the room by themselves.

"Judging by the size of the smile on your face, I think you thoroughly enjoyed that, Mr. Harper."

"I'd be lying if I said that I didn't."

"And what part of that was the most enjoyable?"

Chuck sat and thought for a moment, for he earnestly wanted to give the principal a decent response; he admired and respected her and tried to do right by her.

"It seems like it's a lot easier for me to enjoy watching two people fight when I know that it's not serious. The more serious the fight, the less 'fun' it is to watch. I don't know. I guess I am really just trying to recall how long ago it's been since I was able to get that excited about something of so little consequence."

"Well, the show's over now, and fifth period will be starting in a few minutes."

Chuck took the hint, pushing the chair back from the table to allow himself to stand and leave the room. On his way back to his classroom, he noticed Miles, sitting alone in his own classroom — he'd apparently decided to 'dine alone'. Chuck stuck his head in to say hello.

"You missed a hum-dinger of an argument in the teacher's lounge, just now. Amy Colburn and Darrell Ross." Chuck said.

Miles seemed somewhat less than impressed.

"What were they arguing about?" Miles asked.

"Milk, flour, and cornstarch."

"What?"

"Exactly," Chuck replied. "It was just that meaningless."

Prompt Creation #148 - 1/13/21

"So, you're telling me that's why the wi-fi on my phone never worked at his place?"

"Yes, ma'am. That's what I'm telling you."

Maggie Teague didn't know whether to believe the police detective, sitting across the desk from her, or not. Officer Matthew Buchanan had just finished telling her that she'd never been able to get a decent wi-fi connection in her boyfriend's apartment because of the wires that were planted all over his place — underneath the coffee table, in the cushions of the couch, in the wiring of the lamp on the end table, in the chandelier over the breakfast nook in the kitchen. According to Officer Buchanan, the transmission of the information from those 'bugs', across the same GHz frequency band of radio waves used by wi-fi routers and internet gateways, usually made for bad home wireless networking.

Maggie had always thought that there was something odd about Brad's place. She could stand up from the couch, with a pretty decent wi-fi connection, then walk half of the way to the fridge, only to lose almost all network connectivity, and then, at the fridge, have a signal that was similar to what she'd had standing by the couch. Brad never really seemed that concerned about it. He was always aloof in the way that guys, who have too many irons in the fire, often are. If Officer Buchanan here was to be believed, Brad had several criminal endeavors on the old stovetop –all going at once– and it was a wonder that he'd ever successfully remembered her name even once.

Maggie, when it came down to it, was just trying to understand everything that she'd been told over the course of the last twenty minutes. She'd never thought that twenty minutes worth of information would have the power to overwhelm her mind, but then again, what she'd just learned was enough to short-circuit even the sharpest of brains. This detective was telling her that her boyfriend – probably soon-to-be ex-boyfriend, for she certainly couldn't continue to date a guy who was heading up the largest weapons trafficking ring in recent history in the metropolitan area – was probably only a few days away from going down hard for his crimes. Officer Buchanan seemed genuinely concerned about how Maggie was going to end up coming out from all of this.

"So, Margaret…"

"Please, call me 'Maggie'. No one calls me 'Margaret', not even my mother, and she came up with the name, for heaven's sake."

Officer Buchanan seemed nonplussed, but he started again just the same.

"So. Maggie. I think you've got an opportunity, here, to come out of this smelling like roses."

"What do you mean?"

"Well, we sure would like to know anything that you might know about what Brad has been doing, specifically who he's been working with. What can you tell us?"

Maggie had never wondered what a cow felt like, with some farmer yanking on its udder, but she imagined it felt like this, metaphorically speaking. Nothing like getting used for whatever it is that someone can get out of you.

"Well, Officer, I'm not sure I can be of much help there. As you can tell by the constant look of shock that I've had on my face for the last half-hour or so, I have been pretty much in the dark this whole time."

"Brad never said anything around you about the people that he works with? About any of his associates?"

Maggie thought back, over the course of the past three months, to try to remember anything he'd ever said about what he was doing to make a living, only to become disgusted with herself that she never asked, never concerned herself with the facts. Brad was always very generous with his money –as far as she was concerned– and she'd never even thought to wonder about how someone could be capable of doing that. Sometimes, she thought of herself as so brainless.

"To be honest, Officer, as bad as this might sound, I never really asked any questions."

Officer Buchanan leaned back in his chair, interlocking his hands behind his head and lounging so far back that she thought it was some violation of the laws of physics that he wasn't falling over backwards and getting dumped out of that chair. All the while, he wore a smile on his face that dared the chair to dump him as much as it dared Maggie to question him and his motives.

Prompt Creation #78 - 1/6/21

It's impossible to say whether the marriage between Mr. and Mrs. Blake Tobler –soon to be returning to Blake Tobler and Christine Decker– would have lasted more than five weeks, if it weren't for the bloody knife. The stress introduced into their just blossoming romance, after the discovery of the knife, was quite possibly too much, all by itself, just as a late frost can destroy the entire harvest from even the strongest of fruit trees, just starting to bud. The investigation by the police that followed the discovery of the knife, the legal charges filed by the district attorney's office and the effect of that entire judicial process on the two of them, the media circus that ended up surrounding the young couple during a point in their marriage when they would have preferred to just be left alone; none of these particularly nasty facets of the events of the last month were without significant amounts of stress, and the cumulative stress of all of them put together proved too much for what it was that they –Blake and Christine– were trying to grow.

If you had asked either of them, heading into the marriage, whether or not they'd stand the test of time, of course they would have told you "Yes". Every couple of newlyweds –barring a few of the most peculiar examples, perhaps– gets into a nuptial arrangement because they have intentions of going the distance. Isn't that how it always goes, though; the circumstances of life have laid claim to the romantic fires of more marriages in the history of mankind than the desert has tumbleweeds.

Maybe it had been slightly hasty for the two young lovers to buy the house –that house that was to be their first home– sight unseen from Blake's former best friend (former, as in, previous to a few weeks ago, when Blake threatened the man at gunpoint –a one Simon LeMon, according to records obtained from the Paradise Valley Police Department by the District Attorney of Maricopa County– telling him that he was "never to show his face in that neighborhood ever again"). Simon LeMon was, after all, being investigated in connection to the suspicious disappearance of his former business partner, Abbott Shuster. Of course, Blake and his bride-to-be were both unaware of the myriad reasons for not doing business with Simon LeMon.

But, the house had been priced right, and in Paradise Valley, Arizona, a house priced right is usually on the market for about five minutes.

Maybe they shouldn't have left, the very next morning after the wedding, to head out on their honeymoon — two weeks in the Turks and Caicos Islands of the South Atlantic. Blake was told by his lawyer that the timeline that the police were building, surrounding the disappearance of Shuster, and the alleged use of Blake and Christine's home by LeMon, for multiple meetings between Shuster and LeMon, and some other unidentified business men from Chicago, would have been more difficult for LeMon to manage, had Blake and Christine been around, moving into the house, making renovations, etc..

In the end, they really didn't have any reasons not to trust Simon. Blake and Simon had been friends since grade school, and he'd even been one of Blake's groomsmen in the wedding. But, the friendship —most recently— had become somewhat distant, as the two men were often too busy in their own lives to maintain their bond. Simon was more likely to be involved with his old college chums (Abbott Shuster being one of them) than with Blake, and Blake was an investment broker with hardly enough time to foster a relationship with his fiancé, let alone anyone else.

Despite the fact that Christine and Blake have yet to be implicated in the events that the police and the district attorney are investigating, the process of that investigation —the upheaval to their home and property, the interviews immediately following Christine discovering the bloody knife in the closet underneath the main stairway— took its toll on them. The number of marriages able to successfully weather such an ugly storm so early in the relationship is probably small enough to be mind-blowing.

In the past two weeks, the anxiety and tension had caused the two of them –Blake and Christine– to start to fight, somewhat ferociously. Young people in general, and young couples specifically, often lack the knowledge and grace to forgo seriously damaging each other emotionally when disagreeing with each other. After about a half-dozen such fights, it became obvious that the ship was going to sink, and there wasn't anything that anyone was going to be able to do about it. Christine ended up hiring her own attorney, while Blake was prepared to use the legal services of the lawyer who'd been counseling the two of them through the murder investigation, as a divorce attorney additionally.

The whole disturbance was really just too bad. There was no telling how well the two of them would have fared, otherwise. It's expected that the district attorney will announce the scheduling of the criminal trial of Simon LeMon sometime next week. During an initial meeting that didn't involve Blake or Christine, their lawyers decided that the divorce proceedings ought not to occur within the same time frame as the criminal case, since both Christine and Blake were expected to be key witnesses for the prosecution.

Reportedly, Blake and Christine slept in the master bedroom of their home a total of six times, accounting for the time that they were either on their honeymoon or barred from the property by the investigating police department or creeped out by the fact that someone had allegedly been murdered in their house or at each other's throats and not in the mood to be near each other.

So sad.

Prompt Creation #220 - 1/4/21

Timothy Johnson was probably <u>the</u> geek of his high school class, barring someone else running for the office, and Timothy having to campaign against them. The problem with that is that there isn't a high schooler around, at least not a typical one, who doesn't secretly pine for a smidge of popularity. It's part of the human condition, to want to belong, to want to feel like you've received the acceptance of your peers. Since Timothy Johnson wasn't likely to receive the approval for which he yearned, he'd entertained –in his mind, from time to time– different hypothetical plans for conjuring up some popularity. You could say, it was a hobby of his to occupy his mind with thinking up these different schemes.

When Timothy came up with a particularly plausible concept, he'd hone it and shape it, to try to get the concept to a place where it might actually be something that he could try. But, since Timothy Johnson was still, after all of these years, the geekiest of them all, it suffices to say that none of his concepts had ever developed past the 'prototype stage'.

At one point, he thought that he could manufacture a social media blitz, mostly by coding some bots that he would deploy on different platforms to generate user profiles and then post with those account credentials some positive hype about him. Timothy even went so far as to write the first couple hundred lines of code for creating the bots that he'd deploy from a server in his basement, but it didn't get much farther than that. Timothy wondered whether or not anyone would really take that kind of hype to heart, whether it would result in a boost to his popularity or not.

Timothy also had an idea, a couple of years back, about faking a lottery win for some member of his family, through a manufactured news piece that he could redistribute on the internet and via social media. The news piece, which he would record and doctor with video editing software on his laptop, would publicize the fake lottery win and Timothy would then subsidize the 'new family riches' by using his life savings to spread a little 'wealth' around, making people believe that he and his family were nouveau riche. This plan had a couple of significant flaws in it, not the least of which was that it amounted to just buying the acceptance of his peers — not to mention that Timothy ended up buying a car with his savings, not too long after he thought up that particular plan.

Having a car hadn't made Timothy any more popular. All of his classmates had cars, it seemed. At least, the ones who were old enough to drive.

Of course, it had crossed Timothy's mind to just seek the embrace and approval of the underclassmen, that particular class of sub-humans that would look on an upperclassman —any upperclassman— with a twinkle in their eyes and with love in their hearts, but Timothy recognized that for what it was — a cop out. If he wasn't able to attain the popularity that he was looking for from his own classmates, no other substitute was going to fill the void.

He'd talked to his father about this, on multiple occasions, and his dad seemed to understand in a way that indicated that maybe he'd had the same problems when he was in school. But, his dad came at the problem from a vantage point that was beyond the problem; to him, it was all "you'll get through this" and "their approval isn't that important" and other such nonsense. It didn't help Timothy when he talked to his dad. It really just made him miss his mom even more.

Timothy had never known his mother. For as long as he could remember, it had been just him and his dad. Timothy's mother had left the two of them, not too long after Timothy's birth, at about the time when she realized that being a mother and being a wife sounded more like a death sentence than it did something to which one might aspire. At least, this was the official line coming from Timothy's dad, for as long as Timothy had been asking questions about his mom. Timothy never really had any reason to doubt what his dad had told him about his mother, and where she'd ended up, but it was when

Timothy was missing her the most –when he was especially in need of her care and advice– that he fostered a little kernel of doubt in his heart, doubt about what he'd been told.

At the end of the day, none of it really mattered much, anyway. Timothy didn't have any realistic plans for boosting his social credit. He had a friend or two, relationships that others might consider simple acquaintances, and these weren't really that fulfilling anyway, so –in his most cogent moments– Timothy realized that his dad was probably right; interpersonal relationships, while sometimes rewarding and satisfying, often weren't worth the trouble.

The two of them, like father – like son, were mostly loaners. Since they had each other, the two of them were content with the situation.

Mostly content, anyway.

Prompt Creation #199 - 1/1/21

He stayed over last night.

Beth Silva had been spending most of her business day either sending text messages to her best friend, Amy Vandyke, or staring out the front windows of the Bangor Springs Public Library. As the head librarian, she was basically the person in charge –unless a member of the Board of Directors walked in, heaven forbid– so she had plenty of liberty, to be able to be wistfully staring across the street or texting Amy, as long as the work was getting done. Additionally, Becky Patton, the volunteer intern from the high school, was working this afternoon, and she was a very responsible young lady. Beth knew that she could be relied on for making sure that nothing major fell through the cracks.

That last text message that she'd sent to Amy — Beth knew that it was going to elicit a response.

He who?

Amy was such a kidder. It wasn't as if Beth was spreading it all over town. Amy certainly knew who 'he' was.

You know who.

The desperate staring across Front Street, from the front windows of the library, was an attempt to catch a glimpse of Bruce Randolph, owner and proprietor of Bucky's Bar, situated across the street –almost exactly across the street– from the library. The later it got to be in the afternoon, the better Beth thought her chances might be at seeing Bruce, working away inside of the bar.

Bruce?!?! Are you kidding me?!?! I'm calling you.

Beth looked over to Becky, who was sorting through a shipment of periodicals that had come in for the month.

"Becky, I am going to be taking a call. Can you manage things here for the next few minutes?"

"Sure thing, Ms. Silva. No problem at all."

"Thanks, Becky. And please, call me 'Beth'."

"Sure thing, Ms. Silva."

Beth smiled at Becky's level of youthful zeal. She came out from behind the circulation counter and headed to the back exit of the library, the exit that let out onto the parking lot at the rear of the building. Patrons visiting the library on foot, eight times out of ten, came in the front door; patrons visiting by car, eight times out of ten, came in the back door. Beth left the building and took a seat on a bench near the edge of the parking lot. On cue almost, her phone rang. The caller ID on the phone's screen read 'Amy Vandyke'. Beth answered the call.

"Hey, Amy."

"Don't 'hey' me. You've got some explaining to do."

"Okay." Beth replied, hesitantly. She couldn't quite judge Amy's tone, but it didn't sound entirely positive. She paused, allowing Amy to take the driver's seat in the conversation.
"I guess I just don't know what you see in the guy. He's never really seemed like a great option for you, at least not in my opinion."

"Amy, he's a successful business owner, and a veteran."

"He owns a bar, for Pete's sake. Booze sells itself. It's not like he's entrepreneurial, or anything. And as far as being a veteran, that could be a double-edged sword, sweetie. From what I've heard, he's been a different guy since he came back from overseas."
Beth always had thought that it was one of Amy's least admirable qualities that she was so predisposed to getting information from the town's gossip mill. She'd even broached the subject with Amy, once or twice, to try to discourage her, for whatever that had been worth.

"Amy, you and I both know that you've been in enough bars. To try to pass judgment on any particular bar owner comes off as a little insincere."

"Ouch."

"Sorry, Amy, but it's true. Additionally, while I appreciate your concern on the matter, I am going to proceed, with or without your blessing. I will consider myself warned by you while also releasing you from any responsibility, should things go south."

Beth paused long enough to allow Amy to work through her thoughts on the matter. When Amy didn't make any comments, one way or the other, Beth decided to redirect the conversation.

"So, do you want to hear the details, or don't you?" Beth was really hoping that she did; Beth wanted to be able to share her excitement and giddiness with her best friend.

"Yes, please," Amy responded with an enthusiasm that was a smidge south of exuberant, "tell me everything."

Beth forgave Amy of her disdain, and plowed ahead with the retelling of the events of the night previous, how she'd stayed past closing time at the bar, with Bruce, just the two of them, talking and listening to each other. How he'd offered her a ride back to her place, a considerate gesture. How she'd invited him in. How one thing led to another. The retelling of the story was equal parts an attempt to convince Amy that Bruce was a good choice, and her best effort at reliving the event to try to get Amy to be excited for her.

"Well, it does sound like it was a wonderful evening. I'm reservedly happy for you."

"Thanks, Amy. Listen, I have to get back inside. The work of the head librarian is never done. Becky Patton is in there right now, filling in for me."

"Oh, that's great. Becky is one of my star pupils in Senior English this year. Tell her I said 'hello'."

"Will do. TTFN."

"Ditto."

Beth and Amy had been ending their conversations with each other with 'TTFN' ever since college, when they were paired together as roommates in their freshman dorm at Ferris State. Amy was originally from the Grand Rapids area, while Beth came from the east side of the state. Then, after college, when Beth had landed the job at the Bangor Springs Public Library, and she fell in love with the community, she told Amy every chance she got about how wonderful a place it was. Later, when the position opened up in the English Department at Bangor Springs High, Beth told her about it, and Amy applied, and they both crossed their fingers.

Good friendships are most certainly hard to find.

Prompt Creation #84 - 12/30/20

Just a note → this story, though it shares at least one character and some setting details with the previous story, precedes the previous story by almost three decades.

"So, you're going to need to back up a bit. I don't get paid enough to deal with these kinds of shenanigans."

Abigail Gershwin knew how to handle teenagers. She did it all the time, as the head librarian of the Bangor Springs Public Library. But, there was handling your average teenagers on an average day, and then there was handling Bucky Randolph, Pauley Brachman, and Cyrus Yates. That was a different matter entirely. The three of them, together in her library, usually spelled trouble; let's face it, they weren't exactly 'readers' in the academic sense of the word.

 "Come on, Mrs. Gershwin! Cyrus really has to go!" Pauley begged.

Abigail Gershwin's long-term standing policy on the public restrooms –one for the ladies and one for the gents– was that they were to be locked, at all times, and that the keys were to be kept behind the circulation counter, for anyone who might need to use the facilities. The volunteers complained about this policy all the time, because it relegated them to being glorified "holders of the keys", but Abby was normally able to quash those complaints when she reminded the volunteers that bathroom cleaning could become a part of their list of responsibilities, if they would like it to be.

"Mrs. Gershwin! Please!"

Cyrus Yates was dancing the dance that was unmistakably 'the potty dance'. Even though Abby had plenty of reasons to be suspicious of these three boys, considering how many times they'd pulled fast ones over on her, and elsewhere in Bangor Springs, Cyrus was very obviously in need of a toilet, and –judging by the feverish zeal of his dance moves– he was on the very edge of having an accident.

Abigail reached below the circulation counter, toward the hook that she'd screwed into the underside of the counter, to grab the keys for the bathroom. When her hand came up with the keys, jingling from between her fingers, Cyrus's eyes tripled in size. You would have thought she'd had the latest copy of Playboy Magazine in her hand.

"Here you go, Cyrus."

"Aw, gee! Thanks a lot, Mrs. Gershwin."

Cyrus lunged for the keys, grabbed them from her hand, and was gone like a shot, around the edge of the circulation counter and off in the direction of the restroom. Meanwhile, Bucky and Pauley wandered over to the comfy lounging chairs, near the periodicals, presumably to wait for their friend. Abby went back to checking in the books that she'd retrieved from the overnight book drop container by the back door of the library.

The distance between the circulation counter and the periodicals area was enough distance to allow for Bucky and Pauley to speak in hushed tones and whispers, without Old 'Battle Axe' Gershwin hearing them.

"Do you think he's actually going to do it?" Pauley whispered.

"Well, he got this far, didn't he? Did you see him dancing like he had to pee?!?! I almost felt bad for the guy!"

"Well, Gershwin bought it -- hook, line, and sinker. Cyrus might have a future in acting!"

Bucky cleared his throat, ever so slightly, and nodded his head almost imperceptibly in the direction of the circulation counter. Pauley looked up to see Mrs. Gershwin looking at the two of them. They both stuck their noses down into the magazines that they'd grabbed, trying to look inconspicuous; Bucky had grabbed the Popular

Mechanics for that month, while Pauley was looking at the current Boy's Life magazine.

And then, wouldn't you know it, the two of them ended up getting interested in those magazines. Bucky ended up reading an article about the F-16 Fighting Falcon, written by a journalist from the magazine who'd actually gone up in one of the fighter jets in order to be able to write the article. Pauley knew about that article, and he knew that the article came complete with a cut-out poster of the fighter jet — he knew this because he had a subscription to Popular Mechanics magazine. He'd already read the article, he'd already cut out the poster of the F16, and he'd already hung it on the wall in his bedroom with several pieces of scotch tape, right next to his poster of Alyssa Milano.

Meanwhile, Pauley was reading about the successes of Orel Hershiser, the pitcher for the L.A. Dodgers. Of course, the Dodgers had won the World Series the year before, in large part to Hershiser's fantastic pitching, but Pauley wasn't much of a baseball fan. Even when he was, he was more of a Cubs man; Los Angeles was as far away in the mind of Pauley Brachman as Istanbul.

Cyrus cleared his throat, rather ostentatiously, to startle Bucky and Pauley out of their magazines.

"Hate to interrupt, but we'd probably better get out of here."

"Oh, right." Buckey apologized. He and Pauley ditched their magazines and joined Cyrus as he made his way back to the counter to turn in the bathroom keys.

"Thanks, Mrs. Gershwin. Such a life-saver." Cyrus tossed the keys on the counter without breaking stride as the three boys headed toward the exit door. The keys slid across the counter, almost sliding off, but Abby slammed her hand down on the keys, ending their wayward skid.

About the point in time when the three were free and clear of the library proper, Abigail Gershwin got suspicious enough to want to check the restroom that Cyrus had just used. While she'd initially been convinced that things had been on the up-and-up, there was something about the way that the three of them had exited the building that had been a little suspect. Taking the keys, she went to the door, slipping the key in the lock to unlock the knob, and opened it.

If the bathroom had been larger than a single commode, with a sink and a mirror and not much else, it would have made Cyrus's feat much more difficult. But, as it were, Cyrus probably hadn't had much trouble at all filling the bathroom chest-high with blown-up balloons. As Old 'Battle Axe' Gershwin pushed the door in, to gain entry, the balloons fought against her. When she realized what he'd done, Abby shrieked, closed the door once again, and ran to the exit to see if she could still catch the boys before they'd left the property.

But, they were long gone.

And so, keys in hand, Mrs. Gershwin walked back toward the men's room, stopping by the circulation counter on the way to grab a single paper clip. As she closed the distance to the restroom door, she unbent the paper clip into a single, long piece of thin wire.

She let herself back into the men's room, locked the door behind her, and hoped that she wouldn't ever have to end up explaining to anyone what all of the popping noises were, coming from the inside of that bathroom. All the while, as she was undoing what Cyrus had done, she was cursing the three of those hooligans.

Prompt Creation #77 - 12/28/20

"So, do you know why I've pulled you over today?"

Patrick Hodge wondered how many times the officer in question started off with that line. In the back of his mind, the part that wasn't freaking out about the fact that he'd been pulled over –with his two children in the back seat– was thinking that it's a cheesy line and a ridiculous question. Is it the standard opening line, when an officer doesn't have any idea what else to say, like a pick-up line at a bar serves to assist the nervous stud who would trip all over his tongue otherwise? And, what do people usually say to such a line? Does the person getting pulled over usually say something like, "Yes, Officer, I know exactly why you pulled me over.", or "Gosh, Officer, I've really no idea why you pulled me over."? Does lying, or being honest, get you points, or cost you points, with the officer, one way or the other?

He wondered how many times it was the case that the person being pulled over had no bloody idea why the officer was pulling them over.

"Officer, to be completely honest with you, I have no idea why you've pulled me over this afternoon."

"I'm going to need to have you step out of the car, sir."

Well, this was escalating quickly, Patrick thought. He was under the impression, from his previous experiences and from a general understanding of how things were supposed to work, that you weren't normally asked to step out of a vehicle, not during a normal 'you were speeding' or 'your back driver's side taillight is out' kind of a traffic stop.

"Officer, would you mind if I ask what this is all about? I don't particularly want to step out of the vehicle with my two children in the back seat."

The officer, whose last name was Moody, according to the name badge on his lapel, looked into the backseat, through the driver's side back window, to see Michael Hodge and Cindy Hodge, ages five and two, respectively. He seemed confused to see them there, as if there weren't supposed to be any children in any part of this equation. Patrick wondered why the idea of a father, driving with his two children in the backseat, down a side street in Bangor Springs, was a surprising discovery for this policeman.

"This vehicle has been reported stolen, sir. I pulled you over on suspicion of grand theft auto, in progress."

"Well, I can assure you, Officer Moody, that I am the proper owner of this vehicle. I will get my registration and proof of insurance out of the glovebox, and we can clear this whole thing up, if that's alright with you."

Moody seemed to be thinking about it, and Patrick wondered whether or not police officers were trained on the tactic that a suspect might use, to try to take control of a situation through calm proposals and smooth talk. If they were trained in such things, Moody was either more prone to suggestion than your average cop, or Patrick was more convincing than your average criminal.

"Let's see whatever paperwork you might have, sir."

Patrick leaned over toward the glovebox to grab the paperwork that he always kept inside, in a business-sized envelope. As he made this move, he also took a moment to look into the backseat. Cindy was asleep in her car seat, and Michael was coloring in a coloring book. It seemed that neither of them had noticed what was going on. He grabbed the envelope, extracted its contents, and turned the papers over to the officer, along with his driver's license.

"I am going to, at least, need you to turn off the vehicle and hand over the keys to me, while I take these papers back to my vehicle to attempt to figure this all out."

"Well, I am certainly interested in getting this figured out." Patrick turned off the car, removed the keys from the ignition, and handed them to the officer. "Take as much time as you need."

"I'll be back in a moment."

Patrick watched, through the side rearview mirror, as the officer walked back to his squad car and stepped inside.

With the window still down, and a decent weather forecast in store for the May afternoon, Patrick was glad to not have to worry about any adverse conditions while he sat waiting in his car with his two young children. He looked back at Michael in the back seat just as Michael was looking up to see what was going on, apparently noticing their strange circumstances for the first time. Patrick saw that Michael had finished coloring the page that he was on.

"Daddy, what's going on?"

"Well, I got pulled over by a police officer."

"Why? Were you speeding? Are you going to go to jail? What's going to happen to Cindy and me?"

Patrick chuckled, despite a sense of wary concern, at the questions coming from his son.

"There's nothing to worry about, Michael. I am sure that everything is going to be just fine. Why don't you tell me about what you learned in kindergarten today?"

The distractionary tactic, whether it ended up doing more good for Michael or for Patrick, was just the ticket for passing the time for the two of them, while Cindy snoozed and Officer Moody did whatever officers did, back in his squad car. As the two of them finished talking about all of the wonderful and amazing things that had happened to Michael during his school day, Officer Moody returned to the side of the vehicle. Patrick turned to face him.

"Are you the same 'Patrick Hodge' that just bought the hardware store here in town last year?"

"Yes, sir, guilty as charged." Patrick said, incapable of passing on the pun that was lying right in front of him. "Why do you ask?"

"I sure am glad that someone decided to get that store back up and running, is all. This town has been missing a good hardware store for years now. It's an awful shame to have to drive all the way over to Chester, every single time I need a box of nails or what have you." The officer handed back Patrick's license and his paperwork. The pause, while Patrick waited for the officer to pronounce the results of his 'investigation', grew long enough to prompt the officer to do just that.

"Oh, turns out this whole thing was a big misunderstanding. You see, I pulled up behind you, back when you pulled off of Sycamore and onto Lincoln, and I called in your plate to dispatch, just to have them check. Then, they called back to me to say that the car had been stolen. Turns out, however, that they misheard me when I called the plate in originally. See, just a big misunderstanding."

"I see." Patrick returned the license to his wallet and set the other papers on the seat next to him.

"I sure am sorry about the misunderstanding."

"It's not that big a deal, Officer Moody."

"Please, call me Stan. Stan Moody." The officer reached in through the window to shake hands, and Patrick obliged, although the whole maneuver of shaking hands through a car window was a little awkward.

"At this point, Mr. Hodge, you are free to go. Enjoy the rest of this beautiful day."

Patrick waited for the officer to leave the scene in his squad car before leaving himself, to complete his drive back to his home. He was going to have quite the fish story to tell his wife as to why it took him so long to get Michael home from kindergarten, but he'd tell her the tale. And then, he'd get to the hardware store, a few minutes later than usual, to do the accounting and purchasing for the afternoon.

Prompt Creation #117 - 12/25/20

"He's pretty scary looking, for a mime." Claire blurted out as she looked down at the advertising flier.

"But, the problem is, Claire, you're looking at his casting photo. He looks entirely different with his face paint and his costume on. You won't even recognize him as being the same guy as that picture."

Claire found it hard to believe that any amount –or skillful application– of face paint, that even the finest of costumes, could ever vault a man, who was going to start out looking like this guy, into looking like a decent mime, but stranger things had happened. The truth of the matter was that she didn't really want to go to see another mime and she was just trying to manufacture an excuse for canceling this whole date, an excuse for coming up with a different plan. But, Claire's boyfriend, Charles, was a bit of a mime freak.

And, Charles was dying.

"Read down at the bottom of the flier, all of the reviews."

Claire dutifully looked at the bottom of the flier, to see whether she'd recognize any of the names of any of the people that had written a review of this guy.

"Ben Brantley said he was the best mime in the whole city?"

"I know, right?!?!" Charles called back to her from the other room, "Ben Brantley! One of the most famous writers in the history of the New York Times!"

Claire read another review.

"It says here that Michael Paulson called this guy 'a diamond in the rough'."

Charles came in from the other room, to speak with Claire without having to yell across multiple rooms. As he walked toward her, he was buttoning the top button of his dress shirt. His bow tie, untied, hung around his neck. Claire noticed that the gap between the collar of Charles's shirt and his neck was gaping. He'd lost close to forty pounds since the start of the chemotherapy, and he really didn't have that much to lose in the first place. But, despite the fact that the cancer, and the drugs that the doctors were using to fight the cancer, were both waging war with each other inside of Charles's body, his energy –his joie de vivre– was unassailable. He had a vitality that betrayed the prognosis of his oncologist.

Charles came up to Claire, and gently took each of Claire's hands in each of his, holding them from underneath, supporting them. He looked into her eyes, and Claire was sure that he could see that she didn't want to do this. Claire had as much interest in going out to see another mime as she had in learning to weave baskets underwater. "You don't want to go, do you?" Charles asked her, in a voice that was so pleading and supplicant that he was basically daring her to say that she didn't. Rather, Claire paused and said nothing right away, trying to think of the appropriate way, if there was one, to deny a dying man whatever he might want to do.

"Charlie, why don't we just stay in tonight? We could order sushi from the Blue Ribbon over on 58th, and we could sit and watch Christmas movies on TV. It's supposed to get cold tonight, Charlie, really cold, and I don't know if it's a good idea for you to be out in this weather."

Charles tenderly released her hands, and took a step back, looking her over from top to bottom.

"You're not even dressed. You haven't even started to get dressed."

Claire didn't know what to say, or perhaps it would be more accurate to say that Claire couldn't make a choice between any of the two dozen things that were floating around in her head to say. How do you say no to someone who'll be dead in three months? How hard can it really be to just let someone else have their way all of the time, knowing that it won't be long and you'll have all of the choices left to yourself, because you'll be the only person left to have an opinion on what you should do on a Thursday night in early December. Shouldn't it be enough that Charles wants to do something, and that he deserves the opportunity to do what he'd like during these, his dying days. What happens when your loved one is dying and you don't know how to handle it?

Charles started to unbutton his dress shirt, starting at the top collar button that he'd just finished buttoning. As Claire watched him, the guilt overwhelmed her. She stepped toward him, and stopped him by pressing her hand against his.

"I'm sorry, Charlie. I'll get ready. I'm being selfish, and I ought not to be."

"I don't think so, Claire. It's me who's been selfish lately."

"Now, wait a minute. You can stop right there, mister. You're dying, for heaven's sake, and if there's anyone in this room who should be getting what they want these days, it's you."

Charlie stepped back, this a second step, to release himself from Claire's touch, so that he could finish unbuttoning the top collar button.

"You know, CeCe, I think I like your plan better, anyway." Charlie called her CeCe –Claire Cummins– when no one in the world had ever, and she wondered how many more times she'd ever be referred to as such. A dozen? A hundred? When Charlie died, she would be CeCe no more. That part of her, that facet of her identity, would enter the grave with him. The thought brought the sting of tears to her eyes.

"Christmas movies and a spicy tuna roll, with extra wasabi, could be just the ticket." Charlie reassured her. "We can watch the snow fall when it starts, later this evening. It'll be romantic."

Claire looked into Charlie's eyes, and she could see in them something that hadn't been there just a few moments before, a pall of defeat. Claire wasn't going to have to see another mime –not tonight anyway– and that should have made her happy. But, as Charlie turned to go and change his clothes, she wondered what cost had just been paid for her to have gotten her way.

Prompt Creation #243 - 12/23/20

"Suzie, I need the Benford file right away please."

Susan Hendershot hated to be called 'Suzie', and her boss knew that. He knew that as surely as he knew many other facts about her, having been her boss for about three years now. He called her 'Suzie', nine times out of ten, when he was feeling impatient with her, not that she cared very much about how he was feeling. Most of the time, Tom Amendola was a jerk. Conceited in the way that only small-time lawyers in small town America can get away with being, oblivious in the way that most men in America can't help but being. The later that it got into any particular work day, the harder it was for Susan to put up with the crap that Tom was in the habit of doling out.

"It's on your desk. I set it on your desk right after lunch."

The momentary silence –while he searched for what he was surely going to find, in the place where he'd either not already looked or where he'd already looked and had been too moronic to be successful in his searching– wasn't as long as Susan would have expected. He obviously hadn't searched and didn't believe that the file was there to be found in the first place. Given his poor investigative skills, the world was lucky that her boss was a lawyer, and not a detective.

"I see the file, Suzie. What I don't see is the signature page of the file."

As she was accustomed to doing, as he was accustomed to having her do, she'd done also in this particular situation. After lunch –Susan took her usual half-hour and Tom took his luxurious ninety minutes– she'd placed the Benford file on the left side of Tom's blotter, on the desk in his office. She'd pulled the signature page from the Benford file and set it on the right side of the blotter. She did this because she knew that the signature page was the most important page from any of Tom's files. It was the page that he was most likely to complain about not being able to find, so she made it the most accessible — to make it as unlikely as possible that he would complain.

And yet, here they were; him complaining and her having to listen to it.

"It should be on the right side of the blotter, Mr. Amendola."

"Well, it's not. Could you just come in here, please? I'm getting tired of yelling back and forth."

And Susan was getting tired of it, too.

So, as much as it pained her to think that she was going to have to get up, go into his office, point out the signature page that was most certainly sitting exactly where she'd left it, and exert the energy in showing him what he couldn't see for himself, Susan pushed her chair away from her desk in his waiting room, stood, and made the walk into his office.

It wasn't that this was the worst job in the world, for certainly there were other jobs that would have paid less and would have been more tedious than this one, but Tom was getting more and more insufferable these days. With an increasing frequency, Susan had caught herself thinking that, if he could become a lawyer, without the slightest sign of having a decent level of intelligence, then she had it in her to accomplish the same –or even greater– things.

If the situation continued to be so intolerable, she might take that chance.

Standing in his office, near enough to his desk to see what was on the top of it, but far enough away so that Tom would recognize that she was waiting for his next request of her, Susan waited. She had, after all, done what he'd asked. She noticed, upon looking at his desk, and waiting for him to speak, that the Benford file was where she'd placed it, if not now somewhat off-kilter with respect to the blotter, but the signature page was not where she'd left it after lunch.

Tom looked up to see her standing there, and was then aghast that she wasn't just jumping into the search alongside him.

"So? Where is it? Here's the blotter, and here's 'the right side of the blotter', so where's the signature page?"

Susan recognized in Tom's tone a growing level of frustration at about the same time that she recognized her own frustration level growing. What she could do about his frustration was, unfortunately, not a damn thing. But, that didn't mean that she wasn't fighting pretty hard to keep herself in check.

"Mr. Amendola, I set the signature page of the Benford file next to your blotter, as I always do with signature pages. What happened to it after that, I'm not sure I can say."

"You're not sure you can say? YOU'RE NOT SURE YOU CAN SAY?!?! THAT DOESN'T HELP VERY…"

He stopped, abruptly, as a new thought occurred to him. Susan could see the thinking that was going on in his mind as if his face was betraying a promise not to tattle on his brain, that it might actually be capable of mental processing.

"I came back from lunch, and I saw the signature page where you'd left it. And I thought to myself, 'I won't be needing that until Monday morning', so I ignored it."

"And?" Susan asked.

"And, I started thinking about the Lucas case that I closed this morning in court, what I would need to keep and what I should most likely shred. So, I started doing that sorting."

Susan was afraid of where this train of thought was heading. Nowhere good, she feared.

"I put what I was going to need to keep on file over here," Tom extended his left hand down to the surface of his desk, to the left of his blotter, "and what I wanted to shred over here."

Tom extended his right hand down to the desk, to exactly the place where Susan had set the signature page.

He'd shredded the signature page of the Benford file, Susan was sure of it.

Tom looked up from his extended right hand, up from the right side of his desk, to come to look

Susan directly in the eyes. His face was equal parts 'Oops, I screwed up', 'Man, this is really bad', and an overall sense of confusion that Susan wasn't used to seeing on his face. Tom opened his mouth to speak.

"How could you do this?"

Susan wasn't sure that she heard him correctly, while at the same time being sure that he'd said it.

"Sorry, what did you just say?"

"I said, 'How could you do this'! Come on, Susan! What the hell?!?!"

And then, inside of Susan's mind, she heard it. She heard an audible crack, a snap, as if something that was previously binding inside her head had suddenly let loose. Years later, graduating from law school, she would swear that she had actually heard an audible sound. Years later still, when she made partner at Munger, Tolles & Olson, in downtown Los Angeles, she would still swear that she'd heard a sound. That sound, as she thought more and more about it as the years went by thereafter, came to be known to her as the sound of her chains breaking.

Susan Hendershot hasn't been chained since.

Prompt Creation #75 - 12/18/20

Everyday that Chet Durham reported to work at the
gas station was a day that he thought he could be
using his time and his talent better in other pursuits.
But, truth be told, Chet was your average college
student, spending far too much time playing video
games and surfing social media, and therefore,
those were really the only activities for which he
showed any talent at all, all of which is to say that
those activities –and his mediocre pursuit of them–
would suggest that Chet was the kind of person
that didn't really possess any impressive skills at
all.

But, despite Chet's conviction that his job was
beneath him, being forced to show up to work on
an evening --when a blizzard was brewing outside--
was an even greater blow to his overinflated ego,
greater than showing up to work on any other day
would have been. In Chet's mind, it underscored
the fact that he wasn't really valuable to his
employer, that he was part of a corporate consumer
machine that cared not at all for his safety or
well-being. This made his having to work even
more of a bummer than it usually was.

And, if he was going to be stuck at the gas station
in a blizzard with no one showing up to buy gas –or
any of the other things that the gas station had to
sell– why couldn't he have been stuck with an

employee with whom he would have preferred to spend a significant amount of time? For you see, that's the thing about working at a gas station during a blizzard. No one is venturing out in that kind of a mess, no one with half a brain in their head. So the gas station was dead. It had been a full twenty-six minutes since the last customer had stopped by, and that was just a gas-and-go; they never even came into the store proper.

Instead of being stuck at the gas station with Claire or Monique, who were undoubtedly the two hottest part-time employees on the payroll at the gas station, and both of them students at the same college where Chet was fighting to avoid academic dismissal, Chet was stuck at the gas station with Beverly Hahn, a 68-year-old mother of three, and grandmother of seven, who worked part-time at the gas station, as nearly as Chet could tell, to support the lotto ticket habit that she indulged regularly while she was on the clock. Of course, she wasn't supposed to be doing so; as a matter of fact, she'd been written up multiple times as an employee for playing the scratch-offs when she was supposed to be doing things like sweeping and mopping and cleaning the gas station bathrooms. But, Beverly and the gas station manager were old friends —which is to say that they had been friends for a long time and also to say that they were both old enough to beg the question as to why either of them should be spending some large part of their golden years in a gas station— so any real trouble that Beverly might get into for gambling on the job was likely to be some distance down that particular road.

At the moment that Chet was staring out the front door and front windows of the gas station, wondering how quickly the snow was actually falling, Beverly was on the phone with the manager of the gas station, her old friend Mabel Mosley. Beverly was asking Mabel questions about how long it had to be, with no one showing up to the gas station, before she and Chet could lock up for the night, despite the fact that 8:17 p.m. was not anywhere close to the regularly scheduled closing time for a Thursday evening. Beverly hung up the phone and looked at Chet with a look that told Chet that the two of them were going to be at the gas station till close, come hell or high water.

"She said, 'Stay till close', didn't she?" Chet asked hopelessly.

"Well, come on, Chet. You know what she said. If she'd've told me that we could close the place up, don't you think I'd be wearing a bigger smile than this?"

"I'm going out to shovel around the pumps."

"But, you just did that thirty minutes ago."

"Yep, and in the last thirty minutes, another two inches of snow have fallen. Unless you want to do it?"

Chet knew that there wasn't a chance that Bev was really going to fight him for the privilege of shoveling snow, not when she could stay inside and scratch the flaky silver paint off of several pieces of cardboard while he was out there. Chet walked over toward the break room –which doubled as a stock room– to grab his coat on his way out the front door.

Once outside, the silence struck him in a way that he wasn't expecting. There wasn't any traffic down either of the roads that intersected at the corner of the gas station's property, which in and of itself was pretty astounding, since both of those roads were normally very well-traveled. On top of that, Chet's escape from Beverly was also an escape from that annoying country music that she played on the radio under the counter behind the cash registers. Outside, he didn't have to listen to that crap, and the respite almost made it worth being out in the cold.

He walked over to the side of the building, where the shovel was resting against the exterior wall, exactly where he'd left it when he'd finished shoveling the last time. Chet grabbed it and cleared the sidewalk, perpendicular to the front doors, in four long runs of the shovel from one edge of the building to the other, each time pushing the snow off of the edge of the sidewalk into what was becoming two piles, growing larger and larger, at the periphery of the storefront.

Once Chet finished by the building, he headed out to the two islands of gas pumps, two pumps on each island, and started pushing the snow this way and that with the shovel. He'd done the job enough times this evening alone to be pretty good at it, to say nothing of all of the previous times that he'd shoveled out these four gas pumps. When he was done, he stopped and rested his folded hands on top of the shovel's long handle, supporting himself on it and staring out into the night.

It was in that perfect silence, far enough away from the store and out in the middle of a scene where no signs of human life stirred at all, that Chet was able to hear the snow fall. The sound of a snowflake touching down wasn't a sound to be heard, nor was the sound of a dozen snowflakes doing the same. What Chet heard, as he stood there –holding his breath and struggling to listen– was the sound of hundreds of thousands of snowflakes landing on the top of hundreds of thousands of other snowflakes, already resting on the ground. They fell with a sound like the rustling of tissue paper or cellophane.

For a brief moment, Chet felt small and insignificant, as the roar of the snowfall demanded to be heard.

Prompt Creation #82 - 12/16/20

The clock on the dashboard of my car reads 11:07, which means that I was supposed to have been at work three hours and thirty-seven minutes ago. This morning, however, I just didn't make it all of the way into work.

Rather, I kept on driving.

Now, admittedly, I'd thought about doing this very thing a dozen times, or maybe two dozen times, over the course of the last twenty years, pretty much ever since I started working at my job. As it just so happened, this morning was the morning. I didn't know it, when I got out of bed this morning, that today was going to be the day, but here I am.

I turned the ringer off on my cell phone a couple of hours back. Not because the calls from work continued to come in. At this point, the office has called me six times — in my mind, those calls are pretty easy to ignore. You know how it is, you look over at your phone, to see who the screen says is calling you. Then, because you don't have a particular desire to talk to that particular someone, it's easier to ignore the ringing of the phone, somehow.

The clock on the dashboard of my car reads 11:12.

When I turned my ringer off, it was because the calls were starting to come in from *other* sources, sources that were harder to ignore. So far, my wife has called five times and my mother has called twice.

All told, that's thirteen calls in the last 222 minutes — you would have turned off your ringer, too; trust me.

When I first started out –not turning down the road that had led me to work thousands of times, and instead staying on the other road that would lead me out to the freeway on-ramp– I had some music going in the car. That music, and how much I was enjoying singing along to it, kept me going for the first little chunk of time. Eventually though, I got tired of the noise; it's been silence ever since, silence except for the sound of the engine and the whir of the pavement, passing by underneath the tires.

The clock on the dashboard of my car reads 11:19.

I've only stopped once, since leaving the house — that was about an hour ago, I took an exit ramp off of the freeway, to be able to stop at a gas station. As it turns out, my gas tank wasn't prepared for the amount of driving that I've ended up doing today. With the fuel, I also picked up a bottle of Coke and some Skittles. The teenage cashier behind the counter at the gas station looked even more desperate to bolt than I was feeling.

Part of me is worried about stopping too often; that, if I stop too often, I'll just end up turning around at one of those stopping points. I'm not sure that I want to turn around.

I'm also not sure that I want to keep driving.

At this point, I'm about two hundred miles from home.

The clock on the dashboard of my car reads 11:23.

The problem with being where I am right now is that, as I continue to get further and further away from my home, I am just traveling miles that I am going to have to re-travel, once I come to my senses and turn around. I am getting close to the point where I won't have enough time to get home inside of a normal business day.

I've obviously not thought this whole thing through very well.

I think I'm just running, really. Just trying to break free. Most of the times, over the past twenty years, when I've considered doing this before, I was simply looking to escape, to get away. Most of those thoughts were just fantasies. The thing about fantasies is that they are not meant to be acted upon. They are thoughts that should never see the light of day by being converted into actions.

I don't have any idea what possessed me to actually do it today.

The clock on the dashboard of my car reads 11:31.

The problem is, when I get back, they are going to have some questions for me, questions that will need to be answered. Most people don't do this, I don't think — make random road trips off for a couple hundred miles in some direction for no apparent reason. My behavior today has been the very definition of abnormal. My boss isn't going to care that much, I don't think. My sick leave bank will get charged for a single day of time-off, but I'll tell the people at work some strange story about having to go to such and such a place on an emergency errand of some kind. I'll lie to get around that part of the equation.

But I won't be able to lie to my wife. I am going to have to tell her the truth.

What is the truth that I'm going to have to tell her?

I'm not sure.

The clock on the dashboard of my car reads 11:40.

Escape velocity is the speed at which an object must be traveling along an escape trajectory in order to leave a gravity well. My life is a gravity well. This plan of mine to go off on a drive and to –what? not return? leave it all behind?– was ill-conceived to begin with. I guess I didn't have any right to expect that I was going to be successful leaving it all behind without so much as the slightest of plans.

I'm not even sure that I ever wanted to leave it all behind.

Maybe I need a therapist, or something. Maybe I need some counseling help.

Maybe I just need some lunch.

So, having failed to attain the necessary escape velocity to clear the gravity well, I will fall back down into that well, along the same path that I took trying to get out.

That is, after I stop to get some drive-thru fast food at the next exit ramp.

Prompt Creation #24 - 12/14/20

"He was pretty religious once."

The comment came out of the clear blue, during a period of silence that's not uncommon at a crime scene; during the process of investigating, detectives are looking around and doing the mental work of trying to piece together what they're seeing, what must've happened, and talking tends to be reserved to hushed whispers between partners.

This comment was not a hushed whisper. It was, in fact, loud and exasperate, and it came from a uniformed officer, standing still –and previously silently– off in the corner of the living room.

State Police Detective Albert Nuñez approached the local uni with the intention of giving him a stern talking-to, but that was not how things ended up working out. As he got near enough, Nuñez noticed that the name tag above the badge, next to the officer's lapel, read 'Moody'.

"Officer Moody, would you care to elaborate on that statement you just made, that statement that was loud enough to break the concentration of every detective in this room?"

Officer Moody blushed enough to let Detective Nuñez know that he was embarrassed by his mistake.

"I'm sorry to have caused any trouble, but I am just meaning to add some relevant information to the investigation. Ray Flores used to be a decent man. He used to be a..."

Nuñez caught the eye of the young officer looking past him, lighting on the dead bodies on the floor behind, the bodies of one Ray Flores and one Francine Flores. Moody was ghostly white –hadn't he just been blushing?– and he looked like he was about to lose any food that might be in his system, so Nuñez grabbed him by the arm and quickly led him out the front door of the home.

* * *

After a few minutes of fresh air, with Detective Nuñez standing by his side the entire time, Officer Moody got his color back. Nuñez kind of felt bad for him, probably a rookie, and he could remember back to the days, not so long ago, when he was just a rookie himself. How had a relatively short amount of time led him to the place where he could walk around in a room with a couple of dead people on the floor and he didn't end up reacting like this Officer Moody? Nuñez couldn't remember the last time when he was bothered by investigating the scene of a violent crime. He wondered if that was a bad sign.

"So, Officer Moody, if you are wanting to add to the investigation, now that you're feeling better, why don't you tell me what you know."

"Well, as I was about to say inside, Ray and Francine used to be regular attenders at my church, here in Bangor Springs. Ray was one of the deacons of the church, and Francine had been a part of every funeral dinner in the church basement for like a quarter of a century. But, all of that was before Francine got sick."

"When was that?" Nuñez asked.

"Probably about a year ago, or close to it at this point. Francine was diagnosed with the big C, and the treatments made her so sick that she wasn't really up to much activity. At first, when I noticed that they weren't coming to church anymore, I would stop out here during my patrols, just to check in on 'em. But honestly, it's been a while since I've been out here last."

"So, how long had you known the Floreses, Officer Moody?"

"Ever since I was a kid. Lifelong church members, them and I."

Officer Moody paused in his speaking, and Detective Nuñez waited for him to start up again. When he didn't, Nuñez primed the pump.

"Well, from what we can gather from the scene in there, it looks like a murder-suicide. Certainly, you were thinking the same thing, while you were observing the same set of elements that we were."

"Roger that." Moody responded.

"So, does that seem like something that you'd think Mr. Flores was capable of?"

"Well, you see," Moody began, "that's just the thing. I wouldn't have thought he was capable of that at all. But, I guess, when you're up against the ropes, people do all kinds of things that you never would have thought them capable of. The last time I visited with the Floreses, I didn't even get to see Francine. Ray and I talked for a few minutes, and he mentioned several times how much pain Francine was in. I guess drastic times led to drastic measures."

"Officer Moody, the longer you remain a cop, you will continue to see things that prove that very point. Often times, people resort to extremes when they feel like they've run out of other options."

Nuñez waited for the thought to sink in for Officer Moody. He could tell by the look on the young officer's face that his wheels were turning — it seemed to be occurring to him on a deeper level.

"Thanks for coming out here with me, Detective…"

"Nuñez. Al Nuñez." the detective answered. He reached out his hand, to shake with the local deputy.

"Frank Moody. Thanks, Detective Nuñez."

"Not a problem, Officer. Now, let's get back inside and finish this up. The sooner we are done here, the sooner we can all get home to the people that we love, to let them know how much we care."

"10-4 to that, sir, a big 10-4 to that."

Prompt Creation #70 - 12/11/20

This was the fourth time that it'd happened to Angela in the last month. So, needless to say, she didn't feel the impact of it in quite the same way that she had when it happened the first time and the second time and the third time. As strange as it might be to say such a thing, Angela thought it was getting to be old hat.

Not that anything like this could ever become 'old hat'.

She hadn't told anyone about it. None of her coworkers. None of her siblings — she had three of them: Mike, Melissa, and Andrew. Most certainly, she'd not told her mother. If Angela had told her mother about it, oh how she would have gone on and on about it, probably using that condescending voice that she always used when talking about something that Angela could have avoided, with proper decision-making and a modicum of composure.

But, each time that it happened --this time now the fourth-- she felt the need inside, the need to tell someone, grow just a little bit more. If it kept happening –if this thing kept taking place– she thought that she would eventually get to the place where she'd burst or end up spilling the beans to someone.

She might have considered telling Esme, her cubicle partner at work. Angela and Esme sat across from each other in the data entry pool of the second floor of her office building, each of them mediocre examples of what the data entry division of the company had to offer. Because Angela recognized in Esme the same amateur indifference that she recognized in herself, and because Esme noticed the same about Angela, the two of them were comrades, in a sense. Esme was Angela's favorite coworker, bar none, and she would have told Esme about her secret, if it would have made a difference.

Plus, Esme didn't seem to Angela like the kind of person who would react to this kind of news in a favorable way. Just not open-minded enough.

If Angela decided to tell anyone, it was going to have to end up being someone that she could trust, but also not someone who was likely to be judgmental or scornful. Not that Angela felt like she had anything to do with what was happening, with what had happened –four times now– because she didn't feel like she was to blame…

Or, was she?

The more that Angela thought about it, the more she wondered if she could have been doing anything differently, if she was really to blame at all for this. Honestly, Angela didn't even really understand why it was happening in the first place. It's only natural, of course, for a person to start to look at the whole of their life when something like this happens, to try to see where there might be an explanation. She hadn't recently been eating anything out of the ordinary. She hadn't recently been involved in any strange activities, hadn't recently met anyone new who might be having an effect on her. As much as Angela was trying to find that one thing that would make sense, as the cause of these 'occurrences', nothing had *occurred* to her thus far.

At least, so far, it hasn't gotten any worse. In fact, it had been pretty much the same each time. But, more and more as the days went by, Angela was starting to become significantly afraid of what might be lurking around the corner, of how something like this could end up getting out of hand. What if it started happening with more frequency? What if it started happening in places where people would end up finding out about it?

What was even scarier was the thought that this might be permanent, that she might have to put up with this for the rest of her life.

UGH!

If that ended up being true, if it turned out that she was going to have to continue to put up with *this*, happening periodically, with no end in sight, it would put an end to her love life. Angela chuckled at the thought; isn't the patient on the table already dead when the doctor pronounces the time of death? As a matter of fact, they are — exactly as Angela's love life was pretty much already dead — her love life wouldn't be ended if these incidents continued. But, perish the thought that she might bring some guy back to her apartment one night, just to have this end up happening.

No way. No thank you.

She'd also noticed, especially the last several nights, that it was getting harder and harder for her to get a full night's sleep. Angela was starting to worry so much about the incidents, that her brain was having a hard time shutting off enough for her to be able to fall asleep. Then, during the night, her sleep wasn't quite as deep as it usually was; she'd be awoken more easily, and then she'd have more trouble just trying to fall back asleep. She'd tried chamomile tea, she'd tried melatonin pills, she was even thinking about asking her doctor for a prescription sleep aid, but you know what uncomfortable conversation that was going to lead to…
"So, Angela, any idea why you're having a hard time falling asleep?"

"I absolutely know why, but I'm not sure I can say."

Falling asleep, staying asleep, it was all more complicated than it had previously been.

As she laid there, her snooze period having ended, the blaring noise from her alarm clock jarred her from her deep concentration on the problem, just as the same noise had roused her from sleep ten minutes ago. Angela rolled over –gingerly– and, rather than pressing the snooze bar another time, she turned the alarm off. She was awake anyway. If she stayed in bed any longer, she was going to end up running behind on her morning routine.

This was the fourth time, and each of the times before, it had been exactly this way. 'Old hat' or not, Angela was hardly even disturbed that much by the fact that she was levitating about ten inches above her bed, her blankets and her flat sheet –draping off of her left side and right side– dangling down to the mattress beneath her.

Prompt Creation #55 - 12/9/20

"She was my last chance."

"Now, come on. You don't know that's true. You don't know that's true any more than anyone else knows very much at all about the future."

Bruce Randolph looked at Paul Brachman with a conviction in his eyes that Paul rarely ever saw there.

"I might not know it, Paul, but I feel it. She was my last chance."

Bruce and Paul, as it turned out, were the only two people in the bar at the moment. Granted, the bar wasn't set to open for another three plus hours yet –so, of course, that kept traffic down a bit– but this wasn't the first time that Paul had been in Bruce's bar before opening time.

"She's movin', you know."

"Is that so?"

"She told me after the papers were signed, as we were both leaving Tidey's law office. She said she's thinking about Arizona or New Mexico, some place like that. Said she wants to get a new start."

"Well, you can't get much further away from Bangor Springs than that, can you?"

"I suppose not." Bruce replied.

Paul was at a loss for what to say to his friend, the man who was –most likely– his best friend. As a guy, you so often feel like it's your mission to fix things. To say the right thing. To make the right suggestion. To offer the proper advice. Something told Paul, however, that there really wasn't anything to say that would make any of this any better for his friend.

"Listen, Buck. This isn't the end, it's just the turning of a page. You and Maxine, the two of you go all the way back to middle school, for heaven's sake. It's no wonder you're broken up about the end of such a significant relationship. Anyone would be. But, the page turns, and who knows — maybe the next chapter is better than the previous one."

Bruce looked down at Paul's beer bottle, recognizing that it was mostly empty.

"Another beer?"

"Is the Pope Catholic?"

"That he is."

Bruce reached down underneath the counter, out of habit, to grab a bottle of beer out of a cooler that normally would have been full of them. But, at eleven in the a.m., that cooler was as empty as it had been when he'd grabbed Paul's first beer out of the refrigerator at the other end of the bar. Bruce walked down the way, grabbed Paul a second, and headed back to deliver it.

Bruce stood and Paul sat, there in each other's company for a few moments, neither saying anything, waiting in a comfortable silence for the other to have something to say. The bar gleamed in a way that it could only gleam when it was clean and dry, which it most certainly wouldn't be several hours from now. The jukebox speakers were turned down so low that you needed to strain to try to hear what was playing; tonight, they would be blaring to be heard over the crowd. All of the televisions were blankly staring at the two of them -- later, they would be playing regional and national sports of various types and flavors.

"It was the war, you know. It changed me."

"I know it did, Buck. And Maxine knew it, too. We all knew it, not long after you got home. Some of us adjusted to the 'new you', while others didn't, or couldn't. I would have thought that Maxine could've made the adjustment."

Bruce looked at Paul for a moment, measuring his response in his own mind.

"You know, though, I don't blame her. I never have. I feel like we tried to make it work, but at the end of the day, you can only do what you can do."

"I'll drink to that." Paul said, tipping his new bottle of beer for its first quaff.

The two of them passed the next twenty minutes or so, just like that, sometimes talking, other times, just being present with each other. Paul sipped on his beer while he thought about Bruce, and the fact that Bruce was going to survive this day — the day that he signed his divorce papers — just as he would survive many days to come. Bruce busied himself with this task and that task, each a part of his 'getting ready' routine, all the while thinking about how great it was to have a friend like Paul, who'd be there no matter what.

Then, having finished his second, Paul set the bottle down and pushed himself and his stool away from the bar.

"Well, Lord knows I've got better things to do than just sit around your smelly bar all day. I've got to go."

Bruce deflected Paul's attempt at lightening the mood as Paul turned to go.

"Thanks, my friend, for being here this morning. For being here for me. Part of me knew you would be. When I left that law office and headed this way, part of me knew that you'd be standing by the back door, waiting to be let in. I'm glad to be able to count on you."

"Don't mention it."

Paul had almost made it to the back door when Bruce called out to him a final time, prompting him to turn back around.

"You know, on second thought, she may not have been my last chance. But I think she was my best chance."

"Time will tell, Buck. Time will tell."

Prompt Creation #47 - 12/7/20

Ben and Michael Stevenson were thirteen-year-old twin brothers, sitting on the front porch of their small house on Edgewood Road in Myrtletown, California. They sat on their porch when it got really hot, because their home didn't have air conditioning. Normally, in northern California –especially coastal northern California– you don't need air conditioning much. But, if there was a month where it was going to happen that you felt like you needed to escape the stagnant, hot air in your home in Myrtletown, that month was August. Of all the hours that these two brothers had spent on that front porch, most of them were August hours; at least there was an occasional breeze that would make the humidity on the hottest days somewhat bearable.

Ben and Michael were trying to enjoy the last Friday of their summer vacation, for school was set to start for them on Monday, but it's always harder to enjoy the summer days when they're terribly hot days. Additionally, Ben and Michael both knew that life was going to become very different for them, because they were set to start as freshmen at Eureka High School. Myrtletown is really just a suburb of Eureka, technically speaking, and the brothers had just, a few months prior, been excited to leave their middle school years behind them. But, the familiarity of middle school looks a lot more comfortable, a lot more attractive, when you are staring down the alien world of 'high school'.

Ben and Michael were twins, so they were closer than you'd expect just brothers to be. The two of them had been communicating with each other about how nervous they were, to be heading to high school, and they'd each been doing their best to try to calm their sibling down, taking turns at being level-headed, and alternately, anxious. But, as Monday continued to get closer and closer, it was getting harder for them to be anything other than apprehensive.

The heat wasn't making it any better. The cooling breezes were few and far between.

As the two brothers were sitting on their front porch, in the mid-morning of August 23rd, relishing each small breeze that came in, still with the slight smell of the ocean on each one, Ben was reading a book and Michael was scrolling through YouTube videos on his phone. Neither was talking much to the other one; each of them –at the moment– were feeling concerned about the coming school year. As they sat on opposite ends of their porch, Michael was the first to notice the black sedan coming down Edgewood Road from the west.

As he watched, the black sedan pulled into their driveway.

"Ben, look."

Ben looked up from his book, and saw what Michael had seen. They eyed the car with a peaked curiosity.

Ben noticed that the car was not a late model car. In fact, because Ben was a bit of a car guy —especially classic cars— Ben recognized the car as a vintage ride. A 1967 Lincoln Continental. But, Ben also noticed that it wasn't a standard '67 Continental; rather, it was a bit 'custom', with a lot less chrome than the original car would have had, and also with some very darkly tinted windows. The car had enough black on black on black to exude a certain foreboding quality.

Michael noticed, through the windshield of the car, that the driver was nicely dressed and professional-looking. The man was wearing a dark dress shirt and a similarly dark tie, and he looked to be older, somehow, with hair that was mostly gray and very well-kept. Michael estimated the man's age to be somewhere in the sixties, though children are notoriously poor judges of the age of adults.

The brothers watched the man exit the car and walk toward their porch. He stopped as he noticed the two boys, watching him cautiously from the porch.

"I'm here because I need to speak with Lois Stevenson."

"She's not here. She's at work." Michael replied.

Ben added, "What do you want with our mother?"

The man didn't look like the kind of man who was going to be manipulated in a conversation by a couple of teenage boys. He seemingly ignored Ben's question, instead deciding to reach inside of his coat, into an inside pocket, to pull out a small metal case. He pressed a button on the side of the metal case, and it sprung open. He pulled out what appeared to be a business card. With the card in between his index finger and middle finger, he took the remaining steps necessary to close the distance between him and the porch. He extended the arm and the fingers with the card to Ben.

"Please, just be sure that she gets this."

And, just like that, the man turned, walked back to his car in long strides that got him there quickly and efficiently, and was in and pulling out of the driveway in a matter of just a few seconds.

"So, what does the card say?"

Ben got up and walked over to his brother, handing him the business card. Michael read it.

"A colonel? What would a colonel want with our mother?"

Ben thought for a moment, not just about his brother's question, but also wondering about several other aspects of what had just happened. He reached his hand back out, to take the business card back from Michael, and Michael handed it to him.

"I can tell you this, brother: Colonel…" –Ben looked down to read the name of the man off of the business card– "…Samuel Smithers was NOT driving a military issue sedan. Which probably means that he was not here on official military business."

Michael looked a little confused.

"Then, what kind of business was he here on?"

Ben slipped the business card into his back pocket.

"I don't know what's going on here. But, Mom probably will. And, I'll bet all of my allowance for this week that this has something to do with our dad."

THE END

About The Author:

Phil Brackett lives in his hometown with his wife Jennie, and his three children, Garrett, Lilly, and Sarah. He enjoys his life with his family immensely and has begun the adventure of chasing down a dream as a published author.